T0287013

I'LL
COME
TO
YOU

ALSO BY REBECCA KAUFFMAN

Chorus

The House on Fripp Island

The Gunners

Another Place You've Never Been

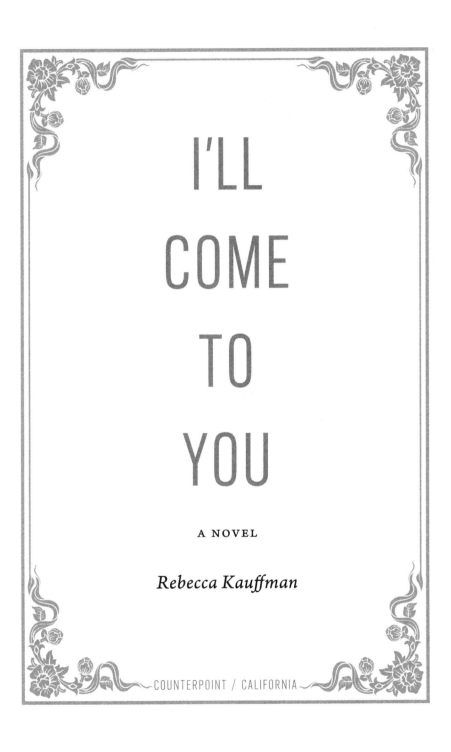

I'LL
COME
TO
YOU

A NOVEL

Rebecca Kauffman

COUNTERPOINT / CALIFORNIA

First Counterpoint edition: 2024

Library of Congress Cataloging-in-Publication Data
Names: Kauffman, Rebecca, author.
Title: I'll come to you : a novel / Rebecca Kauffman.
Other titles: I will come to you
Description: First Counterpoint edition. | California : Counterpoint, 2024.
Identifiers: LCCN 2024035218 | ISBN 9781640096714 (hardcover) | ISBN 9781640096721 (ebook)
Subjects: LCGFT: Domestic fiction. | Novels.
Classification: LCC PS3611.A82325 I45 2024 | DDC 813/.6—dc23/eng/20240802
LC record available at https://lccn.loc.gov/2024035218

Jacket design by Nicole Caputo
Jacket image of wild cat © iStock / the palmer;
green finch © iStock / duncan1890
Book design by Laura Berry
Frame illustration © Adobe Stock / vat2522

COUNTERPOINT
Los Angeles and San Francisco, CA
www.counterpointpress.com

Printed in the United States of America

1 3 5 7 9 10 8 6 4 2

For E

There isn't always someone who wants
you singing to him . . .

—MARILYNNE ROBINSON, *Lila*

I'LL
COME
TO
YOU

JANUARY 1995

ELLEN'S FRIEND SUSAN MENTIONED OVER LUNCH THAT her cousin Gary, a retired bank teller, had announced at their family Christmas that he was ready to date again. Susan added, "And I told him that I have a friend who's in the same boat."

"I hope you were not referring to me," Ellen said.

By the end of the meal though, Susan had talked her into meeting Gary with the assurance that it would be casual. And despite Ellen's initial reluctance, she felt crests of optimism as she lint-rolled dog fur from her red turtleneck to prepare for the date. On the phone Gary had suggested an early dinner at Drapmann's, a family-owned sit-down place that served everything, he said, from a hot dog to a king crab.

A bitter wind made its way up Ellen's nostrils and snow creaked beneath her heels on the short walk across the parking lot. Gary was waiting near the host's stand—Ellen spotted him before he saw her. He had fuzzy gray hair and was slumped on a bench. He straightened up immediately, but only partially, when she entered. He said, "Ellen? I thought you'd be coming from the other way. Susan said you live on Cedar."

Ellen said, "I do. I'm coming from the Salvation Army."

"Do you volunteer?"

"No, just some junk to drop."

"Brrr." Gary gestured outside, then inside. "Shall we?"

They were seated at a nice table next to a window. Their server was a man with a strategically placed Band-Aid covering most of a tattoo on his neck.

Gary opened his menu and put on reading glasses.

Ellen ordered chicken with rice pilaf and Gary ordered the Salisbury steak.

"I always wondered what that was," Ellen said. "Salisbury."

Gary said, "I believe it's a region."

The server returned with a basket of bread, and Gary ordered a bottle of the house red. Ellen rarely drank alcohol but didn't want Gary to think he'd made a mistake, so she accepted a glass when one was offered.

Ellen said, "How were your holidays?"

"Lousy." Gary took off his reading glasses and slipped them into the pocket of his jacket. "Yours?"

"My son and his wife were with her folks on Christmas Eve, then me on Christmas Day. It was marvelous. We have our little traditions."

Gary took a roll from the basket and tore it in half. Steam billowed from it. "Grandkids?"

Ellen shook her head. "Any day, though. They're eager. Trying."

"You're eager too," Gary observed.

"I love children," said Ellen. Because it was so true, she said it again. "I love children."

"I guess so! Susan said you're a school bus driver."

Ellen nodded. "Thirty-five years. It's something to see them grow. Amazing things happen. I'll look at the girl ringing up my groceries or cleaning my teeth and realize I drove her to school when she was five. I'll remember where she lived. I'll remember her name."

"Do they remember yours?"

"I usually have to remind them."

Ellen gazed around the dining room. There was only one other couple seated and they were even older than her and Gary. Slow jazzy piano music was playing. There was a green decorative lantern glowing on each table, giving the place an otherworldly feel. "Do you have children?"

"A daughter," Gary said. "She lives in Florida. We don't talk much. She dates women. She thinks I don't know, but her mother tells me." He took a hefty sip of his wine, then another. "I really don't care who she dates. My daughter, I mean. My ex too, for that matter. As it happens though, my ex is dating an excavator, which I find funny. Enough about me. How do you know Susan?"

"Our sons were good friends in school, and she and I kept up even after the boys were long gone. Her Kenny's apparently become quite the trombonist. He's part of a traveling band based out of Milwaukee and they perform everywhere from Boston to Buffalo. What am I saying? You know this already, you've just spent Christmas with their family."

Gary said, "I didn't know that actually; Kenny wasn't there, and I've learned to tune out Susan's yap-yap-yapping." Gary polished off his glass of wine and poured himself another.

Ellen felt hope dribbling out of her. She peered outside. The sky was the color of wet concrete. Some teenagers were horsing around in the parking lot of the strip mall across the way, drawing pictures in the frosted-over windows of the dry cleaner's.

Gary said, "Susan must have something against you, setting you up on a date with me. That's a joke, you can laugh. But seriously, look at you." Gary flung his hand dramatically in Ellen's direction. "And look at me."

Ellen had no idea what to do.

Gary shrugged. "Sorry."

Ellen excused herself to the restroom, where she did a positive affirmation into the mirror and straightened her collar. For Christmas her son, Paul, had given her a gift certificate to JCPenney, and several days ago she had considered spending that gift certificate on a nice fragrance or a new garment for this date. What a fricking joke! Thank goodness she hadn't worked up the motivation to actually get out and do that.

Their meal had arrived by the time Ellen was back. Gary poked at his meat with the tip of his knife. "Not what I expected," he said. He looked up at her bleary-eyed, like he was submerged in water, then back at his plate.

Ellen said, "That doesn't look like a steak, does it? It looks more like a burger covered with sauce instead of put in a bun."

Gary laughed, and to Ellen's surprise it sounded like a nice person's laugh, hearty and warm.

Gary said, "Tell me about your son."

"Paul and Corinne live in Lamb. Two hours away. You're probably familiar. And like I said, hopefully a little one soon. I really think this is the year."

"You seem confident."

"It's what the lady on the psychic hotline told me."

Gary laughed again. He took a bite. "What do Paul and Corinne do in Lamb?"

"You've heard of Webb's Jam? It's where they both work and where they met. She does office work, handling bulk orders, and he started on the manufacturing line but has risen through the ranks and runs the whole packaging wing now."

"How's that pilaf?"

"Remarkable."

"Good. You know, there was a telemarketer that called up the other day," Gary said. "Her name was Pilar, not pilaf, but your dish there reminded me. Pilar was trying to sell me on some new magazine subscriptions. Nice accent. I got her to tell me about herself a little bit; told her some things about me. She kept trying to steer it back to the sale, of course. So I went along with that. Eventually got out my credit card. I really had her going, she thought she was going to make the sale of the century. The time came to read her my card and just before I was through the whole thing, I hung up. I don't know why I'm telling you this. What the hell? Well anyway, a full hour she kept calling, thinking we'd been disconnected. I probably ruined her whole day. Poor Pilar. How pathetic is that? How mean am I?"

"Good grief. That is mean."

"You've got it now, Ellen."

The server returned to check on their meals, and to Ellen's relief Gary did not order more alcohol.

Once the server was gone, Gary said, "I bet you've never done something mean in your whole life, have you? But you've thought plenty of mean things, surely. Toward your ex, for example. Was there another woman? I bet you've got all sorts of thoughts about the new woman."

Michael had not left Ellen for another woman, at least not that she knew about. In a way, she sometimes thought it would have been less painful if there had been someone else. Instead of that, as far as Ellen could tell, she had gradually just disappeared to Michael over the years—he simply looked at her less and less every day. And when one day last January he finally said that he was sorry but he felt they had drifted too far apart and he wanted a divorce, Ellen did not argue or beg or cry or question him or point out that she had not drifted at all, because even then his face was a fortress. Michael was nearing retirement and didn't make a whole lot more at the insurance office than Ellen did driving buses, but he offered financial support, which she declined. He moved out so that Ellen could stay in their house, and he took one of their two dogs, the bad one, leaving beloved, obedient Rocky with Ellen. Michael also took the guest bed from their home, one of the two dressers, one of the two La-Z-Boys, roughly half of the cassettes. Michael's new house was the same size as the one they had shared, and it sat on a similar plot in a similar neighborhood just nine miles away. It was easy to picture his new life. And he was nice about all of the logistics. The only mean thing he had done was to leave.

But of course Ellen didn't feel like getting into any of this with Gary, so she said of the imaginary new woman in Michael's life: "His girlfriend is such a bitch." She had never said that word aloud in her whole life.

Gary was beside himself. "There we are!" he said. "What's her name?"

Ellen took a sip of wine. "Pam. Pamela. She cuts hair. That's how they met."

Gary said, "Let me guess, she's fifteen years younger than you and dumb as a rock."

"You nailed it."

"So then I'm assuming he wanted the divorce? Don't worry, I got dumped too."

Ellen nodded.

"What does your son think of Pamela?"

Ellen tapped the stem of her wine glass with her fingernails. "Paul doesn't speak to his father ever since the divorce. I get him for the holidays, et cetera."

If only that were true. Paul and Michael were not particularly close—they never had been—but Paul had nevertheless chosen to spend some time with his father this past Christmas. Paul and Corinne had been with Ellen from nine o'clock in the morning until four in the afternoon on Christmas Day, then with Michael for the evening. It was their first Christmas since the divorce; Paul had suggested this arrangement to his parents and Ellen said fine. When the time came for Paul and Corinne to leave her house that afternoon, Ellen said, "Oh no, I forgot to put out the pecan sandies." She insisted on sending the whole batch with them. She assumed Paul would share them with his father, and that made it easier for her to picture their evening. By bedtime, Ellen was in a sorry state and had reached a conclusion: next Christmas must be spent together, the whole family. Splitting up the day this way when she and Michael were only nine miles apart made zero sense. If anyone objected, she had a whole year to persuade them that it was a good idea.

See, Ellen hadn't wanted to argue this point with Susan, but dating obviously didn't make sense for Ellen, because what would she do with a new boyfriend next Christmas if she was already committed to spending it with her family, including her ex-husband?

Gary said, "That's good. At least you got the kid on your side. You deserve that. Webb's Jam, you said? Big company. I imagine that's great benefits."

Gary allowed Ellen to rattle on about Paul for a good while, which perked her up. Then they talked about the new library being built across town and the recent story in the news about the mayor's dog biting some girl on the head, so bad that stitches were required.

When their entrée plates were cleared, the server wheeled over the dessert tray and they both declined.

Gary paid for the meal and said, "Well this was fun. We ought to do it again."

Ellen balked, not wanting to give him the wrong idea.

Gary quickly clarified, "Oh listen, just as friends I mean. I think it's obvious I'm not dating material. I don't know what Susan was thinking. I told her I wasn't ready! But we had an all right time, didn't we? A few laughs. I'd enjoy having another meal with you, Ellen. Just as friends. Maybe somewhere that serves burgers in buns instead of covered in sauce, trying to pass it off like a steak."

Ellen laughed.

"I'll call you later this evening if that's all right, to make sure you made it home and when we're both in front of our calendars. We can set something up, maybe for a few weeks from now."

"That'd be just fine," Ellen said, zipping up her coat. "You've got my number."

"Talk to you later tonight, then."

Ellen didn't know if it was this promise of a phone call later or the prospect of another meal with her new friend or the certainty of the things that awaited her at home, but she felt such a flood of goodwill that she initiated an embrace before they parted ways.

When Ellen got home she let Rocky out, then she noticed the red light blinking on her answering machine, indicating a new message.

"Mom, give us a call," Paul said on the voice mail, "as soon as you get this."

The message had been left over an hour earlier. Ellen listened to it a second time. His voice was buoyant with nerves and it was unusual for him to say "give *us* a call" instead of "me." With a jolt, Ellen thought, *A baby!* It had to be! Anything else, Paul would have just said so. The only time he had ever before left a voice mail like this—breathless and ambiguous—was eight years ago, to tell Ellen that he had proposed to Corinne and she had said yes. A baby! Ellen felt her entire existence transform in one instant. Because what was a child, if not hope? Or more to the point, what was hope, if not a child?

Ellen grabbed the phone and dialed their number. The signal was busy.

They were probably on the line with Corinne's parents, Ellen thought, and she felt an unpleasant twinge of jealousy. She got along just fine with Corinne's family, especially Corinne's mother, Janet, who was very entertaining; if they lived in the same town, Ellen had always thought she and Janet would be great friends. Still, it didn't feel nice to imagine Janet and Bruce receiving this news before Ellen. And since it had been a full hour, they were probably on to Corinne's brother by now, too.

Ellen's thoughts took an inevitable turn, to Michael. Her throat clenched like a fist. She dialed Paul's number again, and again she was met with the cold, toneless pulse of the busy signal.

She was still wearing her coat as she dialed again and again, not waiting more than ten seconds in between. Each moment that passed was a moment that Michael was living in a world where this baby existed while Ellen still lived in a world where it did not.

Finally, in between her attempts, her phone rang. She answered it immediately.

"Hello!" Ellen shouted. "I'm here!"

Gary's voice said, "Ellen? I've been trying for the past hour. Kept getting a busy signal." His words smudged together drunkenly. "I just wanted to make sure you made it home. And then with the busy signal, I had to get through to make sure you hadn't been offed by a burglar or a rapist."

"I'm fine. I'm waiting on a call from my son. He left a message. I think he's calling to say they're pregnant."

"Pregnant!"

"It's not a sure thing," Ellen said. "I must get off the line though, to take his call. Call me tomorrow, why don't you, and I'll let you know for sure then." She hung up before Gary responded.

She felt suddenly furious with Gary, designating him responsible for the fact that she'd missed Paul's call earlier this evening. Rocky was at her side and whining for attention. Ellen bopped him on the head and said, "Oh, shut up."

Ellen peered outside. It was snowing now in fat, oblong, feathery clumps of flakes that smacked and burst into the window. She wondered if there would be fresh snow for Christmas next year when they would all be together, including the new baby. She thought she had better get to work soon on plans so that between now and then she could practice and perfect all the recipes she would serve. Oh, and she could probably get some discounted decorations now; everyone ran great deals on holiday fare through the end of January. Ah! That's what she would do with the gift certificate to JCPenney, she thought happily. She would go tomorrow and snap up as much discounted garland and tinsel as she could get her hands on.

She wasn't mad at Gary anymore. She would be happy to set up another meal. In fact, she might even try out a new Christmas recipe before their next get-together—she could take him some brittle, for example—so that she could get his opinion; he seemed to have lots of opinions about food.

Before dialing Paul's number again, Ellen finally paused long enough to take off her coat and her boots and to consider the magical and mind-bending possibility that the whole time she was trying and failing to reach Paul, and Gary was trying and failing to reach her, someone was trying and failing to reach Gary, like Pilar or the daughter who lived in Florida and dated women.

FEBRUARY 1995

PAUL AND CORINNE SHARED A CAR, WHICH MADE SENSE because they worked the same hours at the same facility. It was rare that there were issues with this arrangement, but today presented one: Paul would work normal hours whereas Corinne had to leave at three o'clock to go to the Tooth Depot to shoot a Valentine's Day commercial—something she had done every year since high school—and she would likely not finish until long after Paul's workday was done. Paul refused to ask a colleague for a ride home; ever since taking on a management role he was reluctant to accept favors. He insisted he would rather wait at Webb's and have her pick him up when she was done even if that meant sitting there hours after his shift ended. Corinne was not thrilled about the timing of the shoot either, but Dr. Penner's office manager Kevin had said it was the only time that worked for everyone else involved.

The morning of the shoot, Corinne asked for Paul's help styling her hair in the back. She instructed him to twist long tendrils around her rusted curling iron until they hissed, which meant the curl was good and done and would stick.

On the drive to work, Paul cupped his palm over Corinne's knee and jiggled it. "Feeling okay?"

Corinne said, "I'm getting too old for this. And possibly too fat for the costume."

Paul turned on the radio and they listened to a report about the launch of the first ever female-piloted space shuttle, scheduled to take place today. Eileen Collins was her name. She was thirty-nine years old. Corinne wondered if she had children.

The local weather report was for squalls and accumulation over the weekend. It had not snowed in a week but had been too cold for a thaw, so the existing crust of snow was dull gray, riddled with tracks and little yellow cones of dog pee.

Paul said, "When I was on the phone with my mom yesterday, she brought up Christmas plans."

"Already? We practically just celebrated Christmas."

"She's determined to have us all at her place, the whole day. Including my dad. She's convinced herself this makes sense."

Christmas existed in another universe to Corinne. The baby would arrive before Christmas; the baby would be smiling and possibly even laughing by Christmas.

Paul said, "I told her to cool her jets and that we'll talk holidays after Birdie gets here."

At Corinne's ultrasound, the tech said that the baby was proportioned like a baby bird at this point, with that big head and curved spine, hence the nickname.

Paul pulled into the employee lot, parked and came around to get Corinne's door, then he offered a steadying arm for the walk in as they crossed some frozen patches on the pavement. Huffing smokestacks loomed at the far end of the sprawling brick building. They entered and dropped their lunch bags in the lounge. The berry-sweet aroma that Corinne typically loved about her workplace had gone overpowering and all wrong in the last month.

Paul said, "See you at noon."

"I'm working through lunch, remember? Since I'm losing an hour at the end of the day. I'll eat at my desk or in the car on my way over." Corinne hung up her coat. "I'll call the main desk here when we're wrapping up and give a message to Shirley, or whoever's covering phones then, so you know when to expect me. I hope I don't keep you waiting long."

"I've got quarters for the vending machine if I need."

When Corinne used the restroom several hours later, she discovered a spot of blood in her underwear. It was the color of rust and smaller than a pencil eraser. At her most recent doctor's appointment they had provided a long list of things she might experience in the coming months that were totally normal. A small amount of spotting was on that list. But this was the first time it had happened and it did not feel totally normal.

By three o'clock though, Corinne had not bled more.

She bid farewell to her colleagues and clocked out.

It started to snow on her drive across town. At first the flakes disappeared as soon as they met the pavement, but by the time she was pulling into the office complex, they had begun to whiten the ground. The sign announcing the Tooth Depot featured a train with teeth for cars.

Dr. Penner was in the lobby when Corinne entered.

He sang, "There she is!" He was wearing a white tie with pink hearts on it. He flapped it around and said, "Look at me, going all out this year."

Corinne congratulated him on his new grandson.

He said, "Lauren's got her hands full now, doesn't she? My God. And I don't gather Phil is much help at all. Don't tell her I said that."

Corinne and Lauren had been best friends in school. The two of them had done the first version of this commercial together as high school seniors, but then Lauren went to college a few hours away and was not available the following February, and she did not move back home. They rarely saw each other or spoke on the phone nowadays, but Lauren always sent a Christmas card with an update and picture of her family. Lauren now had four children.

In any case, it was nice that Lauren's father still called on Corinne to do the commercial by herself every year and paid her handsomely, although it had begun to feel a bit like charity.

Dr. Penner said, "Meet my new office guy, Kevin."

Kevin was a large man with a handsome face and splendid hair, dark and glossy, down to his shoulders. Kevin said, "Hi, Corinne. We spoke on the phone."

Dr. Penner said, "Corinne's been doing this now, how many years? God, has it been ten? Fifteen? I've lost track."

Corinne said, "Me too."

Kevin said, "Come on back, they're getting set up." His tone on the telephone had been demanding, but he seemed nice enough now.

Corinne followed his hulking frame down the hall and found that a lovely and expensive aroma trailed him.

In the operating room, the production team of three young men was hard at work, adjusting the lighting and camera angle.

Dr. Penner explained, "Our usual guy had a last-minute job come up in New York. City. He offered to turn it down to shoot this, and I said, Don't you dare. He's the one who put me onto Brad, said he'd do a great job."

Brad looked at Corinne and said, "The leading lady?"

When Corinne nodded he tossed her a plastic bag and said, "Costume."

In the restroom, Corinne was relieved to find that the cupid costume still fit. She was only in her first trimester and had not gained much weight, but the pink-and-red outfit was corseted around the middle and would show any extra. She sprayed her hair so that it was stiff as a crust.

The room was decorated by the time she returned, with pink and red ribbons draped over the reclining chair and retractable magnifying glass and confetti galore.

She climbed onto the chair.

Dr. Penner pointed at her feet. "You wore different shoes last year."

"Did I?"

"Red heels."

"That's right," Corinne said. "I guess I thought it didn't matter since my feet are never in the shot."

"I kinda liked them anyway."

Somehow it took the team another forty-five minutes to ready everything for the shoot. Corinne sat in the chair for this entire time, under bright, hot lights. As soon as she began to sweat, the cupid outfit took on a uniquely terrible smell. She could not tell if it was her own sweat from previous years and did not allow herself to dwell on alternatives.

Finally the time came for the first take.

Corinne smiled into the camera. "Are you trying to get that smile tuned up for a big date? Whether you're overdue for a cleaning or—"

"Cut," Brad hollered. "How about more . . ." He snapped the air for a word.

From across the room Kevin offered, "Chipper."

"That's it," Brad agreed.

The next take, Corinne got through almost the entire thing, up until the part where Dr. Penner stepped into the shot to give a thumbs-up and deliver his standard line: "Let us get that smile smooch-ready."

A wave of nausea hit Corinne before Dr. Penner had finished this line, and she knew that a look had passed over her face when Brad hollered, "Cut!"

She said, "I know I made a bad look."

Brad said, "No biggie." He regarded her for a moment. "We are going to have to wait for your face now, though."

"My face?" She touched it. "Am I still making a bad look?"

"Now it's too red."

"Oh golly."

Another wave of nausea heaved about inside her.

She and Paul hadn't told anyone beyond family that they were expecting. She trusted Paul's parents and her father to keep a secret, but she'd really had to drill into her mother, who loved to talk, that this news was not to be shared yet. She and Paul had tried so very hard for so very long to get pregnant. It had been such a struggle. Corinne knew of only one other friend who was having a struggle: her friend Jamie, who had no trouble getting pregnant but had had "countless" miscarriages—these were Jamie's words. Before Corinne got pregnant she was privately, shamefully jealous of Jamie and her struggle; Corinne could not fathom getting pregnant so many times you lost count.

Soon enough Corinne's nausea passed and she got through a few successful takes in a row.

But Brad was not satisfied. "I don't know how else to say it other than chipper," he said. "Perky. Sexy."

Dr. Penner didn't seem entirely comfortable with the critique but neither did he step in to defend Corinne's performance.

They did many more takes. Kevin and the production assistants sat in the corner watching. Corinne was exhausted and miserable. She said, "I need to take a break to use the restroom."

Brad said, "Okay, everybody, let's take five."

Dr. Penner glanced at the clock. "I think we need to just go with what we've got. Let's be done." He loosened his tie and turned to Corinne. "You did a good job, hon." But his eyes were on her forehead, then her chin, then the window, where it was completely dark outside now. Corinne thought Paul was probably eating Fig Newtons for dinner.

Brad said, "If you say so. I just wanted to make sure you got your money's worth."

Corinne went to the women's restroom to change but before she had even entered a stall, the exterior door of the restroom opened. She was the only woman in the building. Instinctively, she drew her bundle of clothing to her chest even though she was still wearing the costume and had not begun to unlace the corset.

A voice said through the crack, "Don't worry, it's just me."

Corinne murmured, "Okay."

Dr. Penner said, "I've got to scoot soon and didn't want to leave before saying thanks. Here's your check. You did great, hon."

The door opened another inch, enough for him to stick his arm through it. He clutched a white envelope. Corinne watched as the arm lowered to place the envelope on the floor. His fingers were pink and long.

He said, "Maybe we'll try a different approach next year. Take your time getting dressed. Kevin has paperwork to finish so he'll be here awhile and will lock up behind you. Okay, bye-bye." The pink fingers waggled, waved, and the door closed.

Corinne retrieved the envelope and placed it in her purse.

She changed in a stall, then sat to use the toilet and was alarmed to see more blood in her underwear. Not a lot of blood but a brighter shade of red than she had seen earlier in the day. Her head felt weightless and cool.

She pleaded silently and ferociously with Birdie.

Tears surged from her eyes as she sat there a little longer to see if more blood was going to come.

After a few minutes, she blew her nose very gently. She thought that if she sneezed too hard, the whole world might shatter. But with enough effort she could control what happened next.

She gathered her things and walked out of the room and down the dark hallway.

She was almost halfway to the lobby when she realized she was actually not headed to the lobby but toward the back of the building; she had gotten turned around. While reversing her course she glanced absently into the narrow window of the room nearest her. It was not an operating room but Dr. Penner's actual office, with a big mahogany desk; she knew the room because they had filmed the commercial in here one year.

The light in his office was off but a streetlamp from outside cast a gold luminescence into the room, which illuminated Dr. Penner, seated, in profile.

Corinne's eyes snagged instinctively on something unusual, then snapped into focus.

Her first split-second impression was that Dr. Penner was holding and petting a small, beautiful dog on his lap. Then she registered the reality: Kevin's head was between Dr. Penner's bare legs. Dr. Penner's head was tipped backward and his hands roamed over the magnificent coiffure as it bobbed in his lap.

Corinne felt a lurch and she moved swiftly out of view, in the direction of the lobby, through the lobby, out to her car.

There was a lot of fresh snow on the ground and she barreled through it. She did not know if the roads had been salted or the plows made it through. She also realized she hadn't called Paul.

The trip across town was harrowing in the heavy snow and took an hour instead of twenty minutes. The peril of the drive and focus required allowed for only intermittent speculation about what was happening in her body, and Paul's mind, and Dr. Penner's life. Corinne couldn't decide if what she had seen in his office was funny or sad or okay. She wondered if it was some kind of a struggle.

Eventually Corinne pulled into Webb's, where the tall parking lot lamps shone brightly to reveal that there were no other vehicles. They must have sent everyone home on account of the weather, she thought. They had only done this a few times in all her years with the company.

She trudged through deep snow to the main entrance, which was unlit, and the door was locked. As a long-term employee who occasionally worked overtime, she had a code for off-hours entry and used it now.

She found Paul pacing the long hall that connected the main entrance and the employee lounge. This hall was lined with framed photos of the company founders and some of smiling employees standing watch over the earliest trial batches of jams.

Paul was worried sick. He explained that upper management had decided to shut the whole plant down for the weekend. "If you'd called," he said, "I was going to tell you not to risk the drive, to try and hunker down at the Depot for the night, since the forecast had gotten so bad."

Corinne said, "The phone lines were all tied up when I tried to call. Maybe there's a pole down." She had no idea why this lie had materialized.

"How bad were the roads?"

"It took me over an hour."

"I don't think we should try to make it home tonight," Paul said. "If we slid off we'd be in real trouble. We should stay where we've got heat, sleep on the couches in the lounge, get ourselves home in the morning once the plows have been through."

Corinne agreed.

They made their way to the lounge, where Paul put a Tupperware of water into the microwave for tea.

He said, "How'd the shoot go anyway?"

"It was fine. But I don't think I'll do it again. I'm too old for this crap."

She ate two Butterfinger bars from the vending machine.

They turned on the television and watched a rerun of *The Love Boat*, a Christmas episode. Corinne thought of her mother-in-law, Ellen, talking Christmas plans here in February. This past

Christmas had been so depressing. Ellen had tried to make it nice but seemed like she was on the brink of tears for much of their time together. Then, their evening with Paul's father, Michael, at his home nine miles away from Ellen's was even worse. He had served a confusing meal: sausage patties, potato chips, olives, a frozen pie. He seemed so lost. Corinne didn't understand their divorce. She assumed there was another woman involved but this had never been confirmed, and Corinne would have thought a new woman in Michael's life, even if she was a secret, would have him looking and acting a little perkier. Paul was never in a mood to speculate or discuss anything relating to his parents' divorce. Corinne thought if her own parents announced that they were separating at this stage of life, she would feel like she had been thrown into the Grand Canyon.

They pulled two couches together to fashion a small, uneven bed. Corinne's thoughts roamed about like aimless dark clouds. She couldn't tell if she was feeling cramps or if it was just gas from the sweets.

She listened to Paul's breathing for the next few hours as he fell in and out of sleep. At one point she slept for a bit, too, long enough to dream about another place. When she woke all she could recall of this place was that it was extremely good. Since becoming pregnant she had come to believe definitively in a certain kind of heaven and a certain kind of hell.

At midnight she got up to use the bathroom and check if there had been any more bleeding. Paul did not stir when she stood. With a sinking heart, she was sure she felt damp warmth expanding between her legs. She felt spasms of desperation.

She gazed at Paul and considered waking him but instead turned and made her way quietly out of the lounge. She headed down the dark hall toward the women's restroom. Before she reached it, she passed through the main entrance once again and hesitated in front of the stretch of glass doors to look out into the night.

She thought of Jamie and her countless miscarriages. She felt foolish and cruel for envying Jamie's struggle. She thought if she lost Birdie, Jamie would be the first person she would want to call. In fact, Jamie might be the only person in the world that she would want to talk to ever again.

Corinne peered out of the glass doors to the empty, sprawling lot. The snow had drifted ethereally into peaks that swelled across the land like unknown reptilian beasts. Blustery little tornadoes skittered and swirled about.

It was not like her to keep something from Paul, about Birdie or otherwise. She felt unequivocally supported by Paul; they had journeyed and struggled together. So why, then, had she chosen not to tell him about the horrors of her day? Today of all days, when there was so much to tell! Red shoes; red face; what she'd seen; what she'd felt; what she feared. If she told him anything, she would tell him everything—Paul would want to know it all. But he couldn't, she thought—no matter how accurately she attempted to relay every moment of every day or even if he had been at her side the entire time. In fact, she could even say this now in these words—she could try to describe the distance between what she felt and the words available to convey it—and still that wouldn't be the whole or exact truth. There would always be fissures and chasms. There would always be territory that she would walk alone.

So, here was a terrible secret that rose from this distance and resided in this territory: Corinne did not know if Birdie was going to survive this night. And if this was Birdie's final night, if these were Birdie's final precious hours of life, Corinne wanted them all to herself.

Overcome by an urge, she entered the code to disengage the security system on this door from the inside and pushed it open. She was met with a frigid, wild, howling gale that nearly knocked her back inside and on her bottom. But she pushed forward with greater force to step out into it so that the wailing wind collected her. She felt like she was wrapped in voices. She thought that if she screamed, the scream would have no beginning and no end.

MARCH 1995

I MAY WRITE SOME OF THIS DOWN IN THE NOTEBOOK I
keep, but first I'm getting organized in my head.

In school I enjoyed studying history even though I was a slow
reader. I thought about pursuing this field but was told that most
people who study history end up as teachers, and being in front of
a class wouldn't have suited my personality. So I took a job as a custodian at the Brethren Church because they were advertising work
when I happened to be looking, and I ended up doing this for my
entire career. I took a lot of pride in the job and found it mostly enjoyable. When I retired last year, they replaced me with a lady who
wears her hair in a braid that reaches her butt. I'm not sure if this is
a religious thing or a fashion thing. One day, when I was sure I was
the only one in the building and all the doors were locked behind
me, I thought I must be hearing the voice of God booming through

the back of the sanctuary. It turned out to be a drug addict who had broken in through a window. Well, I guess I can't say for 100 percent certain that that was not the voice of God, because I have lived a life that is unremarkable in every way, yet thinking about it now, sometimes it strikes me that it has been one miracle after another.

There is one thing I cook: chili. Could you guess what the secret ingredient is? It's canned pumpkin.

I had one brother, Harry. We were good pals growing up. Harry fought in the war; I was too young for the draft. I married my high school sweetheart, Janet, who is what I guess you would call a real chatterbox. I'm more a listener myself.

One day when I was young, I was out in the woods near our home, by myself. It was March, like it is now, one of these days where it can't decide if it is warm or cool until dusk, when in one instant it becomes frigid. It was this exact time of day—when it turned— and I was ill prepared for the cold. I was heading in, when I came upon a small nest that was situated low enough in a tree that I could reach it with the help of a stick. I couldn't resist the urge to bat it down for a closer look. It was made of fine materials, twig and hair and feather and moss. It was the most delicate thing I had ever touched. I thought I ought to return it to the tree as best as I could without causing more disruption. But the woods had taken on a dark, funny feel along with the sudden cold, and I was compelled by some urge to destroy that nest. I tore it apart, scattering the shreds on the ground and then even stomping on them. I felt powerful. By the time I had gotten inside, where it was warm and smelled of supper, I was overcome by guilt, imagining the mother returning at a critical juncture on a cold night to find she had no place for her babies. I could not eat that evening; I could not sleep. I decided I must never again do something cruel. I promise you, I have tried to stick to that.

I wonder what sorts of experiences you'll have in your life that will hook inside you. I mean, they'll keep revisiting you (or you'll keep revisiting them; I'm not sure which is more true of the way thoughts happen) until the day you die.

I wonder if you will enjoy school. When I was a child, I had some difficulty learning to read. My teacher thought it would benefit me to be forced to read aloud in front of the whole class often, and I would learn quicker under the threat of humiliation. That was pretty tough on me. Though I guess maybe it did help me to learn quicker.

I have two grandsons, who belong to my son Rob. They live far away, just outside Philadelphia. Rob moved to that area with a friend after graduating high school. The friend had some business ambitions but he ended up in jail. Rob stayed in the area anyway. So I seldom see my grandsons and even less since Rob and his wife split up. He says the divorce was her fault, but I think this might be a lie. Rob has lied about many things throughout his life. I used to hold the lies against him, but then I stopped—I hold nothing against him now—and I just feel sad when I think about him lying. Anyway, I don't know how the custody works, but I know that Rob doesn't have the boys much of the time and this pains me. The last time I saw Rob, his hair was styled with the front long and spiked straight up, and flattened to his head everywhere else. He's in car sales and does very well, apparently. He owns several vehicles. But I don't think he spends more than one or two weekends a month with his boys. He will turn forty in September and has booked a house at the shore for our family to celebrate with him. It was nice of him to do this and must have cost him a fortune, and I love my son deeply, but I'm having a hard time imagining this will be a fun time. Does he not have friends he would rather celebrate with?

I'm amazed by skyscrapers, stalactites, frost, lightning bugs, television, the ocean, dinosaur bones, professional ice skaters, babies, people who speak multiple languages, Venus flytraps, autumn, spring, hot air balloons, bamboo, music, contact lenses, airplanes and pilots, the supposed intelligence of pigs, McDonald's. I wonder if, in the world you grow up in, there will be robots that can sing as beautifully as a person. Maybe these already exist and I just don't know.

I betrayed the trust of your mother yesterday. I don't feel good about it. When Corinne first shared the news she was pregnant back in January, she asked us not to say a word about it to anyone else until the end of March, when she is well beyond what they refer to as the danger zone for miscarriages. Janet had a miscarriage between Rob and Corinne; she had already told loads of people we were pregnant, and I disliked the attention after the loss, so I understand. And last month apparently Corinne had a scare—a little bleeding one day—but nothing came of it; you are fine, thank God. Anyway, when our neighbor Raymond asked me how I was doing yesterday, I felt the need to announce: *My daughter is going to have a baby!* Janet wasn't in earshot, but boy, she would have lit into me for telling. It's not like me to be the one to blab. There's no way it will get back to Corinne that I told.

My little girl is going to be a mother. *Your* mother. This is incredible.

At my grandmother's funeral service, my mother forced me to look at her dead body, and the sight of her powdered pink face terrorized me for a long time. To me it looked like the opposite of peace.

Next week Corinne has an ultrasound that will tell her whether you are a boy or a girl. I am guessing you are a girl; it's just my feeling.

When I was in school and having a hard time learning to read, I had a teacher who made me read out loud often, thinking this would motivate me to learn faster.

One day my brother Harry and I were playing in the fields, when Harry stepped on a nail with a bare foot, and it sunk far in. He stumbled and hollered. I said, "Don't worry, I'll get help," pointing at the neighbor's house, which was much closer than our own home from that location, and I hustled off in the direction of the neighbors, believing I was about to save Harry's life. But I couldn't stop thinking about that nail in my brother's foot, and I hadn't gotten very far when I became queasy and toppled over, passed out. Apparently Harry was watching and saw me sway, then fall, and he had to go for help himself, hopping on one foot the whole way.

For someone who has very rarely had any real conflicts, you'd be surprised by the violence of my dreams.

I don't always feel like myself.

I've not lived a remarkable life. The vast majority of the things I've thought, I've not said aloud.

Soon the time will change and we'll reset the clocks. Spring ahead. Another hour, just gone. Just, gone.

APRIL 1995

ROB ARRIVED HALF AN HOUR EARLY FOR HIS CAREER Day presentation. The smell of the hallway leading to the boys' classroom transported him to his own childhood: bleach and mildew and stewed cafeteria meat and pee and pencil erasers and cheap hand soap. Because he was early, the presentation before his was still taking place. He entered the back of the classroom quietly. Miss Marsh waved. Most of the students were so engrossed that they did not take notice of his entry.

The presenter was an attractive woman in a white jacket. She was utilizing props: a football-sized set of teeth and a laminated poster displaying a diagram of the entire mouth. She had the kids raise their hands to indicate whether or not they had lost baby teeth and how many. Rob watched as Tommy answered that he had lost three; Pete, four.

The dentist explained how adult teeth would differ from the baby ones and the importance of good dental hygiene. She wheeled the overhead projector into place and displayed a slide that she said was a real X-ray of the mouth of someone who did not take care of their teeth. A student raised his hand and said, "My stepdad said in jail they don't let you brush your teeth."

Miss Marsh said, "Okay, thanks Jeremy."

The dentist showed a few more X-rays. Before the final one she said, "This guy had the worst breath you could imagine." She moved the slide into view and it was obvious that it was the jaw not of a human but of a dog. Students laughed.

Many hands shot into the air when she opened it up for questions. One student asked about Laffy Taffy. Another asked the dentist how much money she made.

She finished her presentation by making her way around the room, handing out toothbrushes branded with the name of her practice. When she reached the back of the room, she offered one to Rob and he took it. She was wearing a wedding ring but it seemed like she might be flirting, giving him a toothbrush like that. The notion of flirtation was a welcome distraction from the nerves that had been mounting since Rob had entered the room.

The paperwork about Career Day happened to be distributed on a Friday when Rob was picking the twins up to take them for the weekend. Usually, Liz handled school-related paperwork and logistics. But since Rob received this packet, he saw that the description of their upcoming Career Day included an open invitation to any parents who wished to offer a twenty-to-thirty-minute presentation about their own professional life. Rob brought it up with the boys that weekend and they responded enthusiastically. When Rob saw Liz that Sunday for the handoff, he mentioned that he planned to get in touch with Miss Marsh about penciling him into the schedule.

Liz squinted at him. "You think car salesman is what they have in mind?"

"I'm sorry. Do you think it would be better if you represented the family by going in to talk about how to squeeze a nap in between lunch and a manicure?"

"Okay. Simmer down," Liz said. She licked her finger and turned the page of her calendar. "Ta-ta. See you in two weeks."

Rob thought about his presentation a lot in the days leading up to it, but his thoughts were not organized or even really about the things he would say. Instead he fantasized about the things that the boys' classmates would say to the boys about him after the event. Unfortunately, Career Day did not fall on a Friday when he was scheduled to have the boys, so Rob would have to wait for their visit the following week to debrief with them.

The dentist bid the children farewell and Miss Marsh said, "Next up we have Pete and Tommy's dad, who works in the auto industry. Engineering, is it?"

"Sales," Rob corrected her.

"I must have you confused with one of the dads who came last year. You're at a dealership in town?"

Rob nodded as he made his way to the front of the room, where he snagged a chair, turned it backward, sat down.

He loosened his tie. "Selling cars is straightforward stuff," he said. "I'm just here to answer questions, really."

He expected a lot of hands in the air, like the dentist had gotten. He gave it a little time and said, "Don't be shy. No dumb

questions here. Just dumb answers. But hopefully not that either."
He laughed and the students just stared.

Miss Marsh said, "Maybe you could describe a typical day."

"Sure, if that's what they want. I get in at nine. There's always coffee ready on account of the service guys getting in at eight. We have a team sales meeting, talk through new arrivals, get jazzed on inventory and promotions. Then we divide and conquer on displays if there are any. Banners. Et cetera. Sometimes I have phone calls to return. That can eat up a lot of my day. Then I roam the floor."

Rob tried to ignore a student who had crossed his arms over his desk and laid his head down. Next to that student another was flipping his pencil around his thumb, which had attracted the attention of others sitting near him. Rob raised the volume of his voice. "I wait for buyers and pitch them on what we've got, according to their budget and needs. I facilitate the test drive if they get serious. Pass them off to the financing office if it gets more serious." Rob felt sweat adhere his shirt to his shoulder blades.

Two hands shot up. Rob pointed at one of the kids, who said, "My mom says car salesmen are all lying crooks."

Rob forced out a chuckle that felt like puke.

The other kid lowered his hand.

Rob pointed to him. "Did you have a question?"

This kid said, "That's pretty much what I was going to say, too."

Miss Marsh snapped, "Guys, that's not helpful."

Rob glanced at his sons, who were looking not up at him or at their classmates but at each other, as though for help or just a cue on how they ought to handle this.

. . . .

Lying had spelled out the end with Liz. The dumb thing was, it wasn't even lies about important things. It's not like Rob was having an affair or hiding an addiction to crack cocaine. Rob would lie to make himself look better in the most mundane ways: where he had gotten lunch or whether he'd called his mother. These diminutive falsehoods and exaggerations would just dribble out all day long. It was out of control. Despite the trivial basis of nearly all his lies, eventually Liz said it was just too much—she could not be with him if she could not believe what he said, ever, about anything.

Rob moved out, into a town house that was as big as the family home, where Liz and the boys remained, and in an even nicer neighborhood.

The court stuff got dragged out for many months because Rob was not happy about the custody arrangement Liz proposed. He fought for more time with the boys. But eventually he got tired of fighting. The agreement (that Rob would have every other weekend with the boys and alternate birthdays and holidays) had been made official this past January—in fact, the very same day that Rob's little sister had called to report that she was pregnant.

After delivering her happy news, Corinne had asked Rob if anything was new with him, and he'd said, "Just court stuff. Finally settled custody things with Liz."

"That's good," Corinne said. She hesitated. "Well . . . is it good?"

"Oh yeah," Rob assured her. "All good. I'm good."

Most of Rob's lies sailed out easy as an exhale, but this time he practically choked on the shape and sharpness of that word, *good*.

The town house Rob now lived in was comfortable and he was pleased with the furnishings he had acquired. He had the hardest time sleeping there, though. Rob almost never opened up about personal problems but had mentioned his sleep woes to a buddy. This friend had spent years in the military and offered Rob the tactic he'd learned there for falling asleep as quickly as possible: Step 1: Take five deep, slow breaths in and out. Step 2: Relax every muscle in your body, starting from your scalp and going to your toes. Step 3: Picture yourself in a hammock in a pitch-black room. Step 4: Repeat these words over and over until you are asleep: *Don't think. Don't think. Don't think.*

The guy said the technique worked so well he was usually asleep by the end of step 2.

Rob used this method with varying degrees of success. He also used bourbon and Benadryl. Still, the only nights he actually got good sleep were the four nights of the month that the boys were with him. So sometimes he would do the military tactic but replace the image in step 3 with the image of Tommy and Pete in their little beds here in his house and try to put his mind to rest with this small lie.

Rob smoothed his khakis over his thighs. "People say the same thing about real estate agents, don't they? Jewelry dealers? Any time you're about to put down a chunk of cash on a big purchase, of course you ought to have a healthy skepticism of the seller. We car guys just get a bad rap. What other questions?"

Rob looked at the clock. He had been in front of the class for less than three minutes out of the allotted thirty. He clasped his hands together and spun his thumbs. "You're all eager for the end of the day, huh? Done listening to grown-ups get up here and talk about work, work, work. I get it."

He whistled the *Jeopardy!* tune.

His eyes fell on Tommy, and the expression his son wore stopped him in his tracks. He didn't allow himself to look at Pete. He had to recover this somehow.

He shifted and became aware of the uncommonly large bulge of his wallet beneath his left butt cheek.

Last weekend Rob had gone to a buddy's bachelor party at a strip club up in Mittland. In preparation for the trip, Rob had gone to the bank and drawn out five hundred in cash, in different denominations. The groom-to-be had gotten way too drunk before they even arrived at the club, and the girls seemed disgusted by their group, so Rob hadn't spent a fraction of what he budgeted for; his wallet was still thick with bills.

An idea reached Rob like a rescue flare.

He said to the class: "If there aren't any more questions, I'll get to the most important part of my talk. If you really want some helpful information relating to my field, here it is: Buying a car is expensive, so you'll want to start saving sooner rather than later. That way, when you go to the dealership, you've got enough to put down a large payment on a practical vehicle that meets your needs, rather than bury yourself in a load of debt. That's my career advice, so-called. Because the fact is, no matter what you do for work, whether you're cleaning teeth or flipping burgers, you'll almost certainly need a mode of transportation. So start saving for a car as soon as you can."

He tipped on the chair to reach for his wallet. "What I brought today is a little bit of a start, for you all to put toward your first vehicle." Some heads bobbed up with renewed interest.

Rob pulled the neat stack of cash from his wallet, fanned it out, and said, "It's mostly singles, but there's a couple bigger ones, you can see. Some tens, even a few twenties. Luck of the draw." He got up to grab the large yellow plastic recycling bin in the corner of the classroom. The students watched as he removed the contents, then dropped his wad of cash into it.

"Everybody gets one bill," Rob said. "And when you think about Career Day, remember that the financial decisions you make outside of the workplace—like when you start saving, for instance, or what vehicle you choose to buy—are just as important as the field you go into."

Miss Marsh had a weird look on her face, but the students were all ears—he had their attention now, boy.

Rob made his way around the classroom with the bin of cash. The drama of the picks intensified, with some students getting out of their seats to follow along and get a close view of every choice and every reaction. Tommy loudly addressed Rob as Dad when it was his turn, and moments later Pete did the same.

There was still plenty of time left for Rob to fill by the time he reached the final student, and the next presenter was nowhere in sight, but the kids were in such thrall of Rob that he didn't feel bad about wrapping up early.

After bidding Miss Marsh and the students farewell, Rob stood outside the classroom and listened for a bit. Miss Marsh told the students not to get too attached to their money, that she wasn't sure what had just happened was legal and would need to double-check with the principal before sending the children home with cash. Rob made a face. What a nerd!

It was a perfect spring day outdoors, the air sweet with blooms, the school grounds and rolling hills in the distance boasting exuberant greens. In his car Rob turned on the radio, and turned it up. The shouty voice and surging, aggressive beat of "Self Esteem" by the Offspring matched his mood perfectly. He pulled out of the school parking lot and headed in the opposite direction of his house. He'd taken a half day at work and it was a rare treat to find himself free at two thirty in the afternoon midweek like this. His favorite bar had renovated its patio this past winter, and he thought it would be nice to have a few beers in the sunshine, talk some shit with the bartenders. Bartenders always liked to hear about ex-wives.

He drove past the massive, sprawling furniture warehouse where he had gotten the boys' bunk beds for his town house.

He hollered along to lyrics he mostly didn't know.

He passed the hospital where Liz had given birth.

Liz had recently informed Rob that she was dating a man, whom she described as "a good guy."

Determined to maintain a happy mood, Rob sent his thoughts far from Liz and this good guy, and away the thoughts went, scampering beyond the recent past to the distant past, landing on the memory of Uncle Harry and the year he spent Christmas at their house, when Rob was fifteen. This was an unfortunate misfire—a memory that would make Rob feel far worse, the incident that had lobbed him into a dark hole.

Enough with memories, Rob thought, and pushed his mind forward with what felt like brute muscular force: *I'll call Dad when I get home later.* The last few times he'd spoken to his father on the phone it was like Bruce couldn't even hear him, or was choosing not to listen. Rob wondered if his father had finally given up on hearing anything from Rob that could possibly uplift him. It had been a slew of bad news recently, between the divorce and the custody stuff. Still, why a successful man of nearly forty yearned so deeply for the approval of a church custodian who rarely strung more than two words together was one of life's great or terrible mysteries.

Rob thought optimistically that he would tell his father about Career Day.

He passed the Dairy Queen where he always took the boys on Fridays to kick off their weekends together. On those days it looked like a palace. Today it looked like it was falling to pieces, the roof patchy with bad repairs, all the signs sun-bleached practically colorless.

He passed the park where he often brought the boys on Saturdays. The last couple times they had come, the boys had seemed more interested in trying to ingratiate themselves in groups of older boys than in kicking a ball around with their father. Rob thought maybe he'd set up soccer in his backyard before their next visit, so they could play there together instead of going to the park.

Rob was walloped by the immensity of his needs.

He plowed through some emotion and reached the other side. He thought again of the phone call he would make later to his father and all the things he would say about his Career Day presentation. He would leave out the part about the cash, of course. It probably made sense to tweak a few other things in his telling of the story, too; for example, maybe Rob would say he prepared slides for the overhead projector and brought a bag of branded key chains for the students. He would say that as he left, the children were cheering for him, begging him to stay longer. Halfway down the hall, he could still hear them chanting his name.

MAY 1995

PAUL DIDN'T HAVE THE HEART TO SAY NO TO HIS
mother Ellen's invite to attend the end-of-year faculty and staff
banquet, where she was going to receive a special honor for her
thirty-five years of service. But he didn't like the idea of leaving
Corinne even just for a night, and lately Corinne didn't have much
energy for social gatherings. To his surprise, Corinne was amena-
ble to joining for a night at Ellen's home, and she even expressed
interest in coming to the banquet, too. Ellen had to inquire with
the school about being a plus-two instead of one, and it sounded
like they gave her a bit of a runaround but eventually approved the
request.

Paul and Corinne took off work a few hours early in order to
make it to Ellen's place with plenty of time to get ready for the
event.

Ellen popped out onto the porch when they arrived even
though it was raining lightly, and she gasped with delight when

she saw Corinne's belly. "You were barely showing last time I saw you!" she exclaimed. "Oh, Corinne. And I haven't seen you in person since you found out it's a girl. Hello in there, little lady!"

Paul retrieved their suitcase from the car and Ellen handled the garment bag, insisting that Corinne not lift a finger but instead get herself in and out of the rain right away.

Inside, Ellen pointed out a plate of mini hot dogs wrapped in Pillsbury dough still steaming from the oven and a pitcher of pink lemonade. She said, "I'm showered, so the bathroom's all yours. We have an hour and a half before we should leave."

Paul said to Corinne, "You go ahead with your shower. I need to run out. I'll be back in a few."

Ellen said, "What do you need? I'm sure I have it."

Paul said, "Don't worry."

He got back into the car. In the rearview mirror he watched as his mother stood on the porch until he was out of sight, shielding her fresh hairdo from the rain with her forearms. He had considered stopping by the florist's before getting to his mother's home but decided it would be better if Corinne had more time at home to relax and get ready. He thought his mother probably knew what he was up to, but it would still make her happy.

There was only one florist in town, crammed in a tiny storefront on Main between the CVS and Andre's Shoe Repair. There was not a spot to park directly in front, so Paul circled the block and was parallel parking half a block away, when a figure exiting the floral shop caught his attention.

It was his father, leaving the shop with a lavish bouquet of pink tulips in hand. Michael was wearing khaki pants and a collared shirt and he carried a comically large umbrella. He was headed farther up the block in the opposite direction of Paul—they would not cross paths unless Paul really hustled up there to approach his father, and Paul was not going to do that.

Paul had come to town to visit his mother several times this year but had not seen his father since Christmas. If it was up to Paul, he probably wouldn't have even spent time with his father on Christmas, but Corinne said that without a compelling reason not to, they ought to see Michael on the holiday, even if only briefly. Paul thought this was probably Corinne's way of trying to coax a compelling reason out of him—she was always trying to get Paul to talk about his parents' divorce. He refused, because what kind of a grown man with a life of his own cried over his parents splitting up?

Still, there was that lingering issue of a compelling reason, or the absence of one. "Drifted apart" was the explanation offered to Paul by his father, who first delivered news of their separation over the phone, and this rationale was parroted by his mother even though it was obvious to Paul that these were neither her words nor her experience. Paul had always assumed another woman was involved, though this was not confirmed.

Paul watched with fresh anger, through narrowed eyes, and from a safe distance as his father pulled onto Main, then Chestnut.

But once his father was out of sight and the threat of a spontaneous run-in was eliminated, it struck Paul that the bouquet could be for his mother to celebrate her big night. The more Paul thought, the more likely it seemed that she was indeed the intended recipient; any other occasion for pink flowers at four o'clock on a Friday, this Friday of all Fridays, would be uncanny. In fact, Paul thought, his father was probably headed to his mother's right now to catch her before the event, unaware that he and Corinne were in town.

Paul decided he would take his time getting back to the house in order to let his parents have their moment while Corinne was in the shower. Paul marveled greedily at the idea of his parents sneaking around behind his back; hope was crudely bursting through everything he thought he'd known.

The rain was letting up, so Paul waited a few more minutes in the car until it had stopped completely, then he went into the florist's.

The girl at the counter was scratching her lip piercing. "Here for pickup?"

"I didn't order in advance. Just hoping to get some stems or something premade."

The girl slid off her stool and walked him over to the refrigerator, where she pointed out the options. Pink was Ellen's favorite color but they had none—Paul thought his father must have just now cleaned them out.

Paul picked out a sprightly bundle of yellow carnations and baby's breath, and the girl wrapped them in a tissue paper cone.

Back at home, his mother was fussing around the kitchen, and Paul could hear Corinne's hair dryer going in their room.

He presented the flowers to Ellen and she said, "Oh, dear! They're beautiful." She put them in a mason jar with water. Paul's eyes searched the kitchen and dining areas for more fresh flowers, evidence of his father's visit, and when he found none he thought his mother must have hidden them.

He entered the guest bedroom, where Corinne was wearing only her bra and underwear and was bent at the waist, drying her hair upside down. She startled and straightened up when he entered. She turned off the hair dryer, arched her back, and rubbed her palms over her swollen belly.

Paul whispered, "Guess who I saw at the flower shop?"

"Who?"

"My dad. He didn't see me. He was leaving with a pink bouquet. I assume he brought them over here while you were in the shower, and my mom had him leave before we crossed paths."

"What makes you think that?"

"The timing, with her big event."

"You think he's romancing her in secret?"

"Don't you think?"

"Flowers could be for anyone. It is a Friday night," Corinne pointed out.

"But tonight of all nights, right before her event? And you know how she loves pink. And when he left the florist's he was headed in this direction."

Corinne turned away from him to face the mirror. "You'd better get in the shower."

Paul was disappointed that Corinne didn't share his certainty about this revelation but decided not to push for the reaction he wanted.

The banquet was set up in the school gymnasium, where many long folding tables were adorned with vinyl tablecloths and unkempt arrangements of curled ribbon. The tables were set with pink paper plates and silver plastic cutlery.

Ellen introduced Paul and Corinne to everyone. Paul hated stuff like this, but his mother looked so happy she was about to levitate.

Seats were not assigned and only about half of them were occupied by the time they were informed that the meal was about to begin.

The principal spoke into a microphone, though a loud voice would have done just fine. She welcomed everyone to their annual banquet and congratulated them on the successful completion of another academic year. "We have two honorees this year, but we'll save that for between entrées and desserts. I'll get up and say a few words then. In the meantime, enjoy your meal."

Ellen said, "Oh, I wish she'd get it over with!"

A woman seated nearby said, "You're one of them are you, Ellen?"

Ellen shielded her face like she was embarrassed, but Paul could tell she was tickled by the fuss.

Big bowls of shredded iceberg lettuce were passed around the table, followed by a few dressing options. Lasagnas in aluminum pans were offered as the entrée course. Corinne wolfed down a huge portion and whispered to Paul, wondering if he would initiate seconds so she wouldn't have to be the one to ask.

The principal returned to the microphone and thanked a fourth-grade teacher for her ten years of service. Then she said, "And it is a true honor to offer recognition tonight for thirty-five years of service in our school system. Thirty-five years! This is a rare occasion and a rare treat. Everyone please join me in applause for Ellen Leach, who drives buses for us. Ellen, will you come forward?"

Ellen neglected to remove the paper napkin from her lap before standing, and it fell to the floor.

Paul watched as his mother made her way to the microphone. The principal said, "We have the usual plaque here and this fruit basket and a card signed by the entire staff. And a little something extra for you." She handed Ellen the plaque, a basket full of fruit wrapped in cellophane, and an envelope.

Ellen received these gifts with a dazzling smile. She said, "Should I say something?"

The principal appeared unprepared for this offer but stepped back from the microphone to make way.

Paul watched as his mother positioned the microphone a few inches lower and tapped it. Her voice quaked with nerves. She said, "I just want to say thank you to everyone, and what an honor it has been, and how much I love this work. I hope I can do it for another thirty-five years. What makes this an extra-special night is to have my son, Paul, here tonight and his wife, Corinne." She gazed at them with sheer adoration.

Paul felt color flood his face as many people turned to stare. He silently pleaded with her to be done, and she was.

Back at the table, Ellen opened the envelope and pulled out a gift certificate for thirty-five dollars to Kmart.

"Isn't that nice? Thirty-five dollars because of my thirty-five years, I assume."

Paul said, "Why Kmart? Is that an inside joke or something?"

"An inside joke?" Ellen said. "I don't think so. Just a good place to shop."

The principal stopped by their table a few minutes later and told Ellen that if she wanted, she could take home some full lasagnas since they had several of them left over, unthawed.

Ellen examined the card from her colleagues and kept saying she couldn't believe how many people had signed.

They ate chocolate pudding out of Styrofoam bowls for dessert, then Ellen said, "Corinne, you must be bushed. What a day. Let's go home."

. . . .

In their bedroom, Paul and Corinne changed into their pajamas. "You know what," Corinne said quietly, "I think you're right about your mom and dad. Look at her. Love is in the air."

Paul felt an extension of appreciation for his wife palpably, physically, like a reaching, fattening force. He didn't know when and how to touch Corinne these days—sometimes she seemed to cringe reflexively, and other times she seemed to enjoy being kissed and caressed. He never knew what would happen until he had tried, so he usually proceeded with caution. But in this moment he felt so grateful and amorous that he plopped a big kiss on Corinne's neck, then her mouth, without hesitation. He found the taste of chocolate from the pudding on her tongue. He kissed and kissed, like they were teenagers who were not allowed to do more.

When he pulled away, Corinne laughed like this kiss was a curious but nice surprise. She said, "I'm going to bed, tell your mother goodnight for me."

Paul found Ellen in the kitchen, where she was arranging things in her freezer to make room for the lasagnas. Rocky was curled on the rug beneath the sink but roused when Paul entered the room and came to him.

Paul said, "Corinne's in bed. I thought I'd stay up for a bit."

Over her shoulder Ellen said, "Do you want a beer? I bought a six-pack of the ones you like. They'll just sit if you don't have any while you're here."

She pulled a Labatt Blue from the refrigerator and handed it to Paul. He sat at the kitchen table and sipped the beer.

She said, "I should save at least one of these lasagnas for Christmas, don't you think? I'll make fresh meals, of course, but it's always good to have extra things around that don't take much effort.

I know you and Corinne don't want to talk Christmas till the baby's here. Just thinking aloud."

Paul thought he'd use the opportunity to pry. "At the beginning of the year you mentioned you were thinking of having Dad here. That still the plan? Are you two in touch?"

"Now and then. I did run it by him a while back, the idea of Christmas Day all together here, assuming you'll do Christmas Eve with Bruce and Janet. I just wanted to get your father's thoughts."

"And?"

"And he said that would be just fine." She finished her freezer project and moved on to rearranging the flowers Paul had gotten for her. She emptied the jar, trimmed some stems, then re-placed every flower in the jar, stepping back to assess the shape.

After two-thirds of a beer and this news about Christmas, which he thought all but confirmed that they were getting back together, Paul was feeling so whimsical that he couldn't resist badgering his mother. "That bouquet looks nice, but I think it's missing something."

"Like what?"

Paul nuzzled Rocky's ears. "Like some pink tulips. Do you have any of those lying around?"

Ellen turned to face him. He thought she wore a coy smile when she said, "What do you mean?"

Paul finished his beer and wiped his lips. "Come on," he coaxed. "I know you're hiding flowers somewhere. I know what's going on."

Ellen half-laughed. "What on earth are you saying, honey?" She regarded him with such a quizzical expression that Paul realized in an instant he was wrong.

His eyes fell to his own cold fingers clasped around the empty bottle, which was wet with condensation.

Ellen said again, "What on earth?"

Paul peeled a corner of the foil label off the beer bottle. "I think it was just a dream I had."

"You dreamed I was hiding flowers from you? That's so funny." She turned away from Paul and back to the jar on the counter, where she continued to place stems.

Paul replayed in his head the moment he had seen his father earlier. His father had not looked particularly happy. There was no spring in his step. He had carried the flowers not at his chest where he could admire the colors and enjoy their aroma but slung downward at his thigh, where petals or pollen might be messily deposited. Amid the cruelty of Paul's dashed hopes and his anger over the things he didn't understand, Paul was surprised to feel what was almost a flicker of pity—not for his father but for the recipient of those flowers.

Paul didn't know what to feel for his mother.

Ellen brought the improved bouquet to the table, where she placed it next to the fruit basket. She sat down across from Paul. She removed the cellophane from the fruit basket. The red apples gleamed in the light of the single bulb overhead.

Heavy rain battered the window above the sink.

Nodding toward the fruit, Ellen said, "I know I've told you the story before, about my dad and the banana."

Paul nodded, knowing she would go on with it anyway. It was her favorite story.

She said, "Your grandfather grew up very poor. When he was in school, wealthier children sometimes brought bananas to school. Bananas were expensive back then because they didn't grow locally, unlike apples, which grew in the orchards near their home; he practically lived off of apples, he said. He always wondered what a banana tasted like but was too shy to ever ask anyone for a bite. One year for his birthday, his mother gave him a banana and he said that it was the happiest day of his life." Ellen delivered this line with gusto.

The happiest day of Paul's life, or at least it was the first one that sprung to mind, was learning that Corinne was pregnant this past January after their long struggle. Back in November they had decided to take a pause on their efforts to conceive. It had become so stressful. They agreed they would not worry about tracking ovulation and timing sex for November and December, thinking it would be better to focus on the holidays, then resume their attempts in the new year, a fresh start. Lo and behold, they conceived during this hiatus from trying; Corinne tested positive in January. The joy was staggering.

But something was always pecking at the heels of Paul's happiness. In this case the happiness was corrupted almost instantly by fear of a loss. This fear had diminished as the weeks and months passed; they were now well beyond the presumed danger zone for a miscarriage. But the fear of miscarriage was replaced by the fear of labor and delivery complications and the fear of an unhealthy child. If Paul could extend his optimism beyond that, he imagined a healthy child becoming unhealthy. And if the child remained healthy, what about the inevitable occasion when another person would treat her unkindly, such as with cruel words or by drifting away?

. . . .

Ellen got up to retrieve another beer for Paul. She handed it to him and sat back down. She gazed with pride and pleasure over the array of gifts on the table before her: flowers, fruit, plaque, card with forty-seven signatures, thirty-five dollars to spend at Kmart.

Above all else—smarts or talents or good looks or good fortune—Paul hoped that happiness would come easily to his child. Indeed, for some people happiness seemed to arrive magically and effortlessly, like a little creature that flew to perch on its host's shoulder and devoted its entire life to singing into their ear. In other cases a person had to work like a craftsman to build it painstakingly, tiny piece by tiny piece, and then to protect it from predators of every size and form.

Ellen reached into the fruit basket, withdrew an orange, and sank her thumbnail into the peel. She said, "I think about that story every single time I eat a banana. Any piece of fruit, really."

Paul said, "I know you do."

JUNE 1995

PART 1

JANET CLEANED AND DECORATED THE HOUSE, SLICED the melon and strawberries, readied the tea setup, put the pretzels and Pringles and jelly beans and mints in bowls, and set the table the night before Corinne's shower. It would be only ten ladies in all. Janet had hoped for a bigger group, but it was mid-June, a popular time for family vacations, so many of Corinne's friends and cousins had conflicts with the date and a few others begged out at the last minute on account of childcare issues. Corinne insisted she was fine with a small group, so Janet told herself she must also be fine with it. It helped that there would be pictures of the event regardless of the size of the group. The shower was scheduled for one o'clock, and Janet had asked Corinne and Paul to come half an hour early for family pictures, after which Paul would leave and Bruce would make himself scarce.

Thank goodness for this opportunity for family photos, because the last ones they had taken, this past Easter, were a real disappointment on account of Bruce, whose expression in the photos was dim, his posture catawampus, his graying hair unkempt. Janet intended to keep his condition secret from the kids until after Corinne gave birth to save her the stress during pregnancy, but looking at those Easter pictures, Janet thought, it would be obvious to anyone with eyes that all was not well with Bruce. So in preparation for the shower pictures, Janet talked to him about his face and posture, she got him a new shirt, and she purchased Just for Men hair dye to darken some of the most recent gray patches, hoping that a subtle dye job would go unnoticed in person but would freshen and refine his look in the photos.

Janet had planned to dye Bruce's hair before the morning of the baby shower, but she had read that Just for Men sometimes faded to an unnatural shade after a few washes, so she didn't want to jump the gun by dyeing it too far in advance. Then other things got in the way in the days leading up to the event, and now here they were.

Janet stationed Bruce on a folding chair in the bathroom wearing only his underwear and a rain poncho. It was eight o'clock, plenty of time to get Bruce's hair dyed, get him spiffed up, get herself ready, and do a final touch-up on decorations and snacks before everyone arrived.

Janet put on rubber gloves and mixed the chemicals of the hair dye. She turned on the ventilation fan overhead. She shook the mixer bottle, then went to work, while Bruce paged through an old *Reader's Digest*. She identified the areas on the side of his head that had gone gray most recently—the areas that really showed his age

on those Easter pictures—probed his scalp, and applied the dye in
these places only. She was not going for an all-over job. She did not
want Corinne to notice her father's hair first thing, or ideally at all.
She finished and set the timer, then kissed his nose and said, "I'll
bring you some coffee while you sit."

At twenty minutes, Janet had Bruce kneel over the sink and
she rinsed the dye. The color that drained in the sink looked very
purple, but she knew this was not necessarily an accurate represen-
tation of the actual shade. But after she towel dried Bruce's hair, it
was clear that the color was dreadfully wrong everywhere.

"Oh my," she said. She used her blow-dryer to get a better look,
and it was even worse when completely dry, with large, discrete
eggplant-colored patches. There were purple-stained blotches of
skin, too—the tips of his ears, the nape of his neck.

Bruce stared into the mirror. He said, "Whoa, baby."

"I know." Janet tried not to panic. They still had many hours
before anyone would arrive.

Years ago, Janet had botched her own dye job, then fixed it
herself using bleach, which had first turned her hair a shocking
orange, but a fresh all-over brown dye had fixed this. Sort of. Af-
terward, her hair had been the texture of cotton candy and the
color was a little uncanny under some lighting, but it was still an
improvement. Bruce needed an improvement.

Janet said, "I need to go buy bleach and another box. A different shade."

"Maybe we should just shave it all off."

"A shaved head? You'd look like a convict. I'm going to get a
nice, neutral shade of gray. Forget trying to make you look younger.
We'll just make you look normal. At this point, that's the best we
can hope for."

At the CVS, Janet found a bleach kit on clearance, so she was in high spirits on her return.

Bruce was in the kitchen, eating a bowl of Golden Grahams and watching the news on the miniature television set that lived above the microwave.

Janet sang, "Take two," and they returned to the bathroom.

She had used hair bleach on herself only the one time, so she read through these instructions before starting in. She warned him, "This might hurt. And it's going to look very wrong before it gets right."

Janet applied the bleach. After a while, Bruce complained of a stinging feeling. Janet said, "I know, honey, but we've got to leave it a little longer. See, we're trying to lift all the color, and that takes time."

"Is it supposed to feel like you set my head on fire?"

Janet looked at her watch. "Nine more minutes. I'll go get you a Pepsi with ice. That will cool you down."

By the time she got back, Bruce's eyes were watering and his face was deeply flushed. Janet said, "Are you crying?"

"No. My eyes are just watering."

"That's called crying," she said. "Here, let me rinse you."

Bruce's hair was a truly extraordinary color, a golden, glowing orange. His skin was so red. Janet guided his head under the faucet and rinsed with cool water. Bruce winced and she apologized.

She wrapped a fresh towel around his head and kissed him, then she scrunched the towel.

"Now we just have to apply this fresh shade of gray, see here?" She showed him the box which featured a handsome man on the front who could not have been more than forty years old. "I know this isn't quite what we were going for. I thought it would be so nice if you had some brown like when you were younger, but this will be the next best thing. See how handsome this man is? Just like you."

She unwrapped the towel and was horrified to discover a few blisters and scarlet patches of burned skin. "Oh my Jesus," she gasped.

Bruce turned to look in the mirror but she stopped him—he could be sensitive to the sight of blood. "I don't want you to see the color without the fresh dye. Wait till it's fixed. Stay put."

She got the jar of Vaseline from beneath the sink and applied it to the burns. She was so close to falling to pieces. She couldn't tell how badly she had hurt him. He seemed uncomfortable but okay. He wasn't crying anymore.

She looked at her watch. Somehow it was ten o'clock already. She looked at the box of gray hair dye. Dare she try to dye this hair, applying yet another set of toxic chemicals to this head? She thought, *I must*, and then she thought, *I can't*. There was too much damage to his skin—she couldn't possibly run the risk of exposing him to more.

She said, "Change of plans. Haircut time."

"I thought you didn't want to do that."

"I didn't. Desperate times, though. This is beyond repair."

"I thought you said the gray dye would fix it."

"I changed my mind, okay?" Janet spoke tersely. "Your hair's got the worst texture, I should have known it wouldn't hold dye right." She thought he would be less likely to realize she had made some terrible mistakes if she took this tone.

She got out the clippers. It all had to go. She had never seen Bruce with his hair shaved clean down to the skin, but this was the only way.

Her despair deepened as she got closer to the scalp and saw the extent of his burns. The more hair she removed, the more burned surface seemed to materialize. There were blisters and patches of skin so raw that tiny spots of blood oozed from them. Furthermore, the patches of eggplant-colored dye on his skin from earlier were still prominent. His head looked like a prop from some violent horror movie. What to do?

Before long, an idea reached her. It might not go over well with Corinne, who could be so critical, but would still result in good photos. Janet's friend Linda's husband had lost his hair to chemotherapy several months ago and wore a toupee nowadays. It was not convincing if you knew him before the cancer, but it looked nice nonetheless and could have passed for his real hair if you didn't see him often. Janet recalled Linda saying they had gotten it at the wig shop in the mall, where they were impressed with the selection and the prices.

Janet would tell her daughter she'd tried to give Bruce a little trim and messed it up. She'd say, "Trust me, the wig is better than the alternative." Corinne would think it was weird that her father was wearing a wig regardless of the explanation, but Janet thought, *It wasn't always all about Corinne!*

Janet didn't know what her son-in-law, Paul, would think. She never knew what Paul was thinking.

At the wig store, Janet asked the young woman at the counter where to find men's options in gray. Then she thought, Well, if it was going to be obvious Bruce was wearing a wig anyway, she might as well go for something more youthful. There was no reason to get a wig that could potentially age Bruce. So she said, "Actually, salt and pepper for a man if you've got that. Some gray, some brown. A distinguished look."

The girl, whose name tag read PANDA, said, "Sorry to say, we're out of stock in men's wigs with combination hues. It'd either be all gray or all brown."

Janet really had her heart set on salt and pepper. She said, "Show me what you've got for women's in salt and pepper."

Panda showed her a few options for women's layered looks featuring mixed brown and gray hues. Janet pointed to one said, "I'll take it. I'll cut it myself, like a man's. I've been cutting my husband's hair for decades."

"Are you sure? Synthetic won't behave the same way real hair does, for cutting. Also if this is for a man, the hairline on this is different than an actual men's wig would be. See where it falls on—"

Janet said, "Trust me, Panda. I know what I want."

On the way home, Janet thought that if Panda was that girl's actual name, her mother must be a real loon.

Janet was trying not to pry about names with Corinne and Paul. She had opinions, of course. She had named Corinne after her own aunt, who eventually took Janet in since Janet's mother did not want a child, not at all. That had been made clear in a number of ways. Apparently the labor itself lasted for days and was horrendous and did a number on Janet's mother, physically and mentally. So then Janet was passed around quite a few times from infancy, including to some foster homes, before landing with Aunt Corinne at the age of twelve. Aunt Corinne meant a great deal to

Janet; she represented, for lack of a more sophisticated explanation, the first time Janet was on the receiving end of love.

Janet wasn't sure who represented what to her daughter.

Back at home, Janet put the wig on Bruce and was pleased to see that the salt-and-pepper hues did resemble Bruce's hair as it had looked in the not so distant past.

But cutting it into a man's style was a different matter. Panda was right—this hair did not do at all what Janet wanted it to. The cuts all came out so blunt it was impossible to achieve a well-blended line. And since the part was off-kilter, she didn't have a good gauge for length and accidentally went way too short with the bangs instead of sweeping them to the side.

Janet looked at the clock and looked at Bruce; it was noon and a geriatric Prince Valiant sat before her. She was in a wretched state. Her mind whirred. Bruce was not a wearer of hats and only owned one, a yellow winter cap of knit wool. She retrieved it but couldn't bring herself to put in on his head. That wool would irritate his scalp even worse than the interior of the wig and it was June, eighty degrees outside. If anything screamed *not well* it was wearing a winter hat in June.

It was twelve fifteen, then twelve twenty, then twelve twenty-five.

Janet said, "Oh, hell." She came over to the couch, wig in hand, and sat next to Bruce. "We'll just tell them the truth. That I wanted to dye your hair and messed up and that you'll just sit out the family pictures. We'll do pictures with our whole group another time. We've still got two months before the baby comes. By that time, your scalp will be all healed up and your hair will have grown back some. We'll make sure we get some great shots with the baby when you're looking more yourself. For now, you just relax. You can en-joy watching the photo shoot."

"Photo shoot?" Bruce said. "For who, again? Lolly?"

"Lolly!" Janet cried, and she sprang up from the couch. She stood over him and clapped her hands over his cheeks. "Bruce, this is a baby shower for your daughter, Corinne! She's having a baby. Lolly is the danged cat that's been dead for ten years! Jesus Christ, Bruce."

Bruce touched his mottled scalp, then withdrew his fingers like he expected to find something on them. "I've got it now," he said. He smiled. His head tipped to one side and the smile lost its luster, then disappeared altogether.

Janet said, "Never mind." She grabbed the wig and Bruce's hands and pulled him up off the couch. "Never mind. Just, here, let's go down to the basement. Come on."

She hustled him over to the stairwell, then down it. There was an old flowered love seat in the basement that faced a television set. She threw a fleece over Bruce's legs.

She said, "Do not come up these stairs, do you hear me? You stay put. Watch a few programs, take a nap, enjoy some peace and quiet. I'll run and make you a sandwich quick, and there's that jar of pickles."

She would tell Corinne and Paul that in the hustle and bustle of the day she had completely forgotten about the photo shoot and had sent Bruce out with a book to spend the afternoon at a café; he wouldn't be back until four o'clock in the afternoon. They'd get a few photos, just the three of them. The full family shoot would have to wait.

. . . .

Janet found herself torn between relief and mounting concerns in the coming hours because Bruce did not emerge from the basement for the entire baby shower.

By the time everyone but Corinne had left, around three thirty, Janet's fears had compounded. What if he had died down there? What if she had killed him with the bleach, seeping into his brain? Would she stand trial and go to jail? Janet despaired at these vague and unrealistic possibilities and then at the alarming reality: that she could no longer predict or understand or ignore the depth of Bruce's cognitive decline.

Last year when the memory loss first became apparent, Janet had done some reading. There were a number of possible conditions with different outcomes. It seemed as though it could be extremely serious and terrible, or not. The trajectory in the coming months would provide vital information. So Janet observed. The initial progression seemed slow. Then suddenly it was not so slow. Then she knew she ought to schedule him an appointment to get it assessed and diagnosed—that it would be not merely irresponsible but a moral failing not to do so—and she really had intended to. But with Corinne's pregnancy news in January it seemed better to just ride things out awhile and avoid the upheaval sure to accompany an official diagnosis; it had even crossed Janet's mind that someone might suggest he'd be safer and better off somewhere other than here at home. Now, though, things were completely out of control. Janet lived daily with the feeling that she was radically alone and under constant threat of both exposure and catastrophic change.

Corinne offered to help her mother clean up and Janet insisted she leave right now, right away, to get home and rest. As soon as Corinne was gone, Janet made her way down to the basement in a panic.

She found Bruce asleep on the love seat, the open jar of pickles at his side. He had turned on the radio to listen to some classical music, and Janet turned it off. She went to him and curled up next to his warm body.

He stirred, then woke slowly. He scratched his head and grimaced. "Why are you crying?" The sight of her tears seemed to upset him. "What happened?" He looked like he was going to cry, too.

"Now don't you start," Janet said with a sniff.

The wig was on the ground in front of Bruce's feet and Janet tried to kick it, but it caught on the toe of her shoe and stuck there like a stubborn animal, even as she tried to shake it off. Janet started laughing. As soon as Bruce registered her laughter, he started laughing, too.

"You crazy man," Janet said. "Do you even know who I am?"

Bruce laughed harder. "Of course I do."

Something about the way he laughed made it feel like he not only knew who Janet was but he understood her elementally—in both her components and her entirety—and his deterioration was one long and elaborate trick he was playing on her. She clung to this idea with all her might. She said, "You got me good, Brucie. You really had me going."

JUNE 1995

PART 2

LIZ'S NEW BOYFRIEND, DONNIE, CO-OWNED A HOUSE IN the Outer Banks with his siblings and had dibs on June, so he and Liz had conspired to spend the whole month there with the twins. When Rob pointed out that this was a gross violation of the custody arrangement, Liz offered as consolation some extra time with the boys before and after this trip. She even had the gall to invite Rob to join for as much of the trip as he wanted, supposedly with Donnie's blessing.

Rob had crossed paths with Donnie a few times since Liz and Donnie had gotten together, and that always went fine. Donnie, a librarian, was about as exciting as 1 percent milk—not at all the sort of guy Rob pictured Liz falling for. In any case, vacationing together was an absurd proposition. But Rob was a few drinks deep when the invitation was extended, feeling antagonistic and superior, and he decided to accept. He rationalized this move to Liz with a lie: that he had a sales conference in North Carolina at the end of month anyway, so it made sense for him to extend his trip to join them for the final days of their vacation.

Donnie's beach house was ramshackle but located in a nice area, far from traffic and commercial riffraff.

Liz met Rob at the door.

"You packed light," she observed.

"Did I?"

"That dinky duffel for a whole week of work in Charlotte and your time here?"

"Big suitcase in the trunk," Rob said. He expected some further interrogation or open acknowledgment of his lie, but she dropped it.

She looked great—tanned and calm. Rob was torn on whether to resent her Zen or be grateful if it meant she might be nice.

"Where are the boys?" he asked.

"Down at the water with Donnie."

Rob stepped inside. The place was dark and it smelled of meat and mold.

Liz showed him to his room, a vaulted nook with a twin mattress on the floor. He'd share a bathroom with the boys, who were in bunk beds across the hall.

Rob looked out the window at a wooden walkway that disappeared over a hulking dune, which obscured a view of the shore.

Liz said, "Make yourself at home." She brushed hair back from her face. She was wearing a blue bikini under a white mesh cover-up. "There's Zima in the fridge, I know you like those."

"I do."

She added, "And sandwich stuff if you're hungry. The Swiss is all for you; the rest of us prefer cheddar."

Rob thought this was either very thoughtful or a trap.

After she left the house, Rob took a shit in a toilet so tiny it felt like an act of hostility toward anyone expected to use it.

Then he changed into his swim trunks, did some sit-ups, opened a Zima, and headed to the beach.

From the crest of the dune Rob could see to the shore. Liz was in a chair with a book on her thighs.

Rob had a brief choking sensation when his eyes rested on the twins, who were in the water, throwing a football with Donnie. Rob watched this for a few seconds, calibrated his agony, and jogged down the sand.

Donnie saw Rob before the boys did, and he pointed their father out to them. The twins peeled out of the water to Rob, pumping their arms and hollering as they loped through the sand.

They tried to tackle Rob, then stood and panted, huffing hot air and shaking water from their ears.

Rob looked up and down the beach, which was abuzz but not crowded. A lifeguard station nearby was occupied by an attractive girl whose long legs fell from her perch.

Donnie approached with an outstretched handshake. His swim trunks were covered with pink parrots. Rob had a better body. He shook Donnie's hand. "You been having good weather?"

"All except for the rain last week," Donnie said. "Oh, I guess you probably got that too, since you were in the area."

Rob adjusted his sunglasses.

Donnie said, "I wish I had a nicer room to offer you. It's pretty bare bones here. Our family's used to it, but."

"All good," Rob said.

The afternoon was oddly pleasant. Donnie was very laid-back. His conversation was enjoyable—he asked leading questions about subjects like Rob's vehicle recommendations and favorite sports teams. He said how much the twins had talked about Rob over the course of the past few weeks; apparently they could not wait for Rob to get there. Rob was pleased to hear this, because now that the initial excitement of his arrival had passed, the boys displayed little interest in playing with him. It was okay; Rob was glad to put his feet up.

Eventually Rob got into the water and splashed around with the boys for a while. They had gotten much bigger since the last time they had all been at the beach together. Now when Rob tried to throw them into the waves, they didn't go very far.

Rob got back out of the water. Donnie was tapping a frisbee against his thigh. "Care to toss a few?"

Donnie was better at throwing and Rob was better at catching. Liz was either sleeping or pretending.

Donnie got out the paddleball set next, and it took awhile but eventually the two of them settled into a rhythm and were able to volley the ball in the air for a long time. They got so good that they decided they had better start counting. Hundreds of hits back and forth without the ball touching the ground, then they reached a thousand. Liz and the boys started to watch and count along.

Rob and Donnie worked up a tremendous sweat with this

activity. When the ball finally dropped into the sand, they got into the water to cool off.

Donnie ran his hands through his thin hair and said, "I don't know where you find time to hit the gym, working the hours you do."

"I do most of my exercises at home," Rob said. "It's all about your mentality. Dedication. I can walk you through my routine later if you want."

When they started to pack their things to head into the house, Liz said to Rob, "Donnie and I thought we'd head out to a seafood place for dinner so you could have some time alone with the boys."

Rob had sort of been hoping that he and Donnie might man the grill together or something. "It's no big deal; one happy family, right? You should stick around."

Liz said, "I'm dying for something other than burgers or frozen pizza. And the boys will be happy to have you all to themselves. We'll be back in time for me to put them down."

While Liz showered, Donnie showed Rob how to work the grill and told him to help himself to fixings for burgers and frozen french fries and anything else that looked good.

Rob preheated the oven for the fries and emptied them onto a sheet.

After Donnie and Liz had gone and the meat was cooked, Rob and the boys assembled burgers over the counter, then sat together at the table. As Rob lifted his burger for the first bite he noticed that the boys were not preparing to eat but instead had gone silent, their heads pointed at their laps.

He said, "Earth to Tommy and Pete."

Pete shushed his father.

Tommy peered at him with one eye. "We're praying, Dad."

"Suit yourselves," Rob said. "I'm gonna dig in before it gets cold." He chewed noisily. "Mm-mm-mm. Yummy."

When the boys finally wrapped up, Rob said, "So that's a thing. Every meal?"

Pete said, "And before bed. We're Christians now."

"I see," Rob said. He was torn between caring and not caring. "As of when?"

Tommy said, "Last weekend. We went up to the front of the church here when they asked if anyone wanted to give their life to Jesus."

"You've been going to church here?"

Pete nodded. "Donnie goes to church back at home, too. We're going to start going with him."

Rob said, "Ohhh-kay." He made big eyes and took a big bite. He'd grown up attending church. He had no issue with faith, he just hadn't maintained his—it had grown inconvenient at a certain point, a thing he no longer wished to factor into his life, so he discarded it painlessly, like a garment he'd outgrown. He said, "What's your mother got to say about this?"

"She went up to the front of the church, too," Tommy said, "to give her life to the Lord."

Rob guffawed. "Did she now?" He picked up a french fry and chomped into it. He burned his tongue, threw the fry back onto his plate and said, "Shit!"

Pete scowled. "Maybe you should ask Jesus into your heart, too."

Rob fanned his face then took a drink and swished cold water around his mouth.

Pete added, "It's easy."

"I'm good." Rob went to the freezer and pulled out an ice cube, which he placed on his tongue. "But thanks a bunch."

The twins were on to a new subject by the time Rob returned to the table.

He put the TV on for them while he cleaned up the meal, then they played Chutes and Ladders, then read books together. It struck Rob that ordinarily around this time of day the boys would be tearing around the house, screaming and socking each other, but tonight they seemed content to focus on quiet activities. Rob thought they must be growing up. Or maybe it was that they were Christians now.

When Donnie and Liz returned, Liz put the boys to bed and Donnie went out to the patio to clean his fishing equipment. Rob didn't know what to do with himself so he took a shower—his third of the day—then went to bed.

In the morning Rob got to witness the full prayer ritual over breakfast, but it wasn't anything interesting, so he couldn't come up with any commentary or response.

Down at the beach, Rob and the boys built a giant turtle out of sand.

They went in for sandwiches at lunch, then the boys wanted to fish with Donnie. Rob stayed at the house to help Liz clean up because he didn't know anything about fishing.

As she put condiments in the refrigerator, she said over her shoulder, "How are your parents?"

"Dad's weird. Mom's mom."

"Weird how?"

Rob wished he had words for it.

Several weeks earlier when Rob was on the phone with his mother and Bruce had declined yet another opportunity to get on the phone to say hello, Rob said to Janet, "Is something going on with Dad?"

"Nope. Why?"

Suddenly, Rob was too embarrassed to ask why his father rarely wanted to speak to him anymore. It felt pathetic to take notice of such a thing.

"Seems like all my friends' dads are starting to see problems," Rob said. "Medical stuff, I mean. I just figured with Dad being in his seventies now, I'd check."

"Picture of health," Janet said. "Not as good as me, though. He's soft around his belly nowadays as I'm sure you've noticed, but that's nothing new."

Janet redirected the conversation to her own exercise routine— twenty minutes on the recumbent bike every night—and then Rob told her about his.

"They must be so excited for Corinne's baby," Liz said.

"I guess."

"I wonder how the shower went. Corinne said it was going to be last week? With your mom hosting?"

"Who said what now?"

"Corinne said on the phone, the last time we spoke."

"You talk to Corinne?"

"It's just been since she got pregnant. She's called a few times to chat."

"That's weird."

"No, it's not."

Rob squinted. "You guys were never close."

"We always got along. Anyway, didn't mean to bring up a sore subject. Didn't realize your sister was one."

"She's not. I just don't know what you two could possibly find to talk about."

Liz opened a bottle of Sprite with a slow twist to release some hissing carbonation.

Rob was starting to get mad. "So what's with the church stuff? I hear you and the boys went up for an altar call. Proper conversion, sounds like. Donnie's got you all aboard the Jesus train?"

"I told you he was a good guy when we first started dating."

Rob snorted. "So that's all it takes to be a good guy in your book? Traipse to the front of a church and recite some words? *God is great, blah-blah-blah*—poof—good guy? Or good lady, in your case."

Liz returned his sarcasm with a measured look. "You don't need to be in front of the church. Asking the Lord into your life and being transformed is something you can do in the privacy of your own heart any time." Liz sipped her Sprite. "You know all this; you were raised in the church. I don't know why you're being so nasty."

"I'm not being nasty. I just think it's fake. Say a few magic words and you're good as new? It's just kind of stupid. Lazy thinking."

"I don't want to fight." Liz fiddled with the cap of her Sprite. "Everybody's been getting along so well. And I wish you wouldn't be mean about Donnie. It's extra mean because he doesn't have a bad word to say about you. Last night at dinner he mentioned what a great father you are. And that he can see the two of you becoming real friends."

Rob scratched his chin, for something to do. He thought Donnie probably did make a good friend. Rob didn't have many of those. He had loads of buddies. But not many who seemed to actually give a shit or actually listen to what Rob said, the way Donnie did.

"Anyway," Liz said. "Your sister's scared of labor. If you must know what we talk about."

"Oh." Rob was quiet for a moment. "Were you?"

"I'm sure I would've been if I'd gone full term. I think it would've hit me in the final months. As it was I didn't have time—I—well, you remember."

Rob's head tipped and rolled backward toward the past and he let it hang there by its tendons, as he stared up at the ceiling.

The twins had come two and a half months early. Middle of the night. It was terrifying. They didn't even have a crib set up yet.

Tommy almost didn't make it. It was so, so close.

Rob and Liz had never told the boys about their birth and the close call. Come to think of it, Rob and Liz had never even had much of a conversation about it themselves. After Tommy's health stabilized there was still a stressful and seemingly endless stint in the hospital until both boys were big enough and strong enough to be sent home. Liz practically lived at the hospital for those months. Rob had to go back to work. Then the boys came home and there was no time for talking. And anyway, what was there to say about nearly, but not, losing a child? Well, Rob thought, they could have held each other more. Oh well. Whatever. Whatever. Whatever.

Liz stayed at the house for an afternoon nap and Rob decided to head down to the beach since the boys would probably want to swim after fishing.

Yellow flags were posted at the shore and Rob noted that there were few swimmers. He approached the lifeguard, the same girl who was there yesterday.

He cupped his hands around his mouth. "Hello up there!"

She gazed idly down at him through iridescent lenses then back to the water.

Rob said, "Yellow flags mean proceed with caution?"

"Moderate risk with the riptide. Experienced swimmers only."

Rob stood there a little longer with his hands on his hips and gazing out at the water, but it didn't seem like she was a talker, so he left her side to unfurl his towel onto the sand nearby and proceeded to the water.

He felt the strong current right away around his ankles but it didn't strike him as anything he couldn't handle.

He hurtled into water up to his waist and did a little dive into a whitecap to wet his hair.

Out of nowhere, the sand beneath him was gone, and for a panicked moment he flailed.

Then he kicked his torso up to the surface to find a floating position and when he found purchase he hurriedly paddled in toward shore before the next large wave approached. Once he felt safe, he felt giddy.

Behind him, a whistle chirped. He turned to see what was up.

The lifeguard had left her station and was standing at the edge of the water, whistle at her lips, flotation device in one arm, gesturing emphatically to him with the other.

Rob put his hands in the air, waved them around, and waggled his hips, feigning distress, with a goofy smile.

She did not stop gesturing.

Rob called, "Ya caught me! Just a quick dip. Only wading now, though. Safety first. See?"

She just kept cycling her free arm around like a robot then she sounded the whistle again, this time sustained and with force.

Rob turned toward the water to make sure she was not addressing someone farther out, but he was the only one.

He muttered, "Christ's sakes," and walked toward her.

When he got close, she barked, "I told you! Experienced swimmers only."

"What makes you think that disqualifies me?"

"The way you handle yourself."

Rob laughed. "I appreciate your close attention."

"Just stay out of the water until the yellow flags are down, okay?"

"And if I don't?" Rob edged a toe back in the direction of the water. He meant it to be endearing.

"I'll report you to the police station right there at Bender's Cross and you will be issued a legal citation." She didn't wait for Rob to respond before spinning away to return to her station.

"You're no fun," Rob called after her.

He walked to his towel, dried off, and lay down. He could not enjoy himself though, thinking what a dumb and embarrassing man he was and wondering how many people on the beach had witnessed the whole thing. So he headed back to the house.

When Donnie and the boys returned from fishing a while later and went down for a swim, Rob had no guarantee the lifeguard's shift would be over, so he could not join them. He was hurt that the twins didn't beg.

Dinner and bedtime passed without incident. Rob kept mostly to himself, complaining of a headache. They all pitied him for that.

He lay awake in bed for a long time, feeling alone and sorry for everything and sorry for himself. He thought about the possibility that Liz and Donnie would marry. He was assaulted by anxiety. He thought of his uncle Harry, and his father. He felt sick in a deep way like his heart was defective, made wrong and different, not red and robust but grayish and oblong.

In the morning Rob made an excuse to leave early because he knew lots of cleaning would be required to ready the place for Donnie's sister, who would arrive later that day.

There was traffic on the single-lane road leading away from Donnie's beach house. Rob's mind wandered while he was stuck at a standstill.

Liz's words about the altar call rattled about in his head. Rob considered, too, what his son had said: *It's so easy.* Was it easy? And more to the point, was it real? Dare Rob imagine that he, too, might be made good by something easy?

Unable to come up with a compelling reason not to, Rob prepared the words and rehearsed them in his mind, then spoke them aloud, asking Jesus to come into his heart.

He shivered and braced himself for a change.

To his astonishment, as soon as the words were out a buzzing feeling shot through him and settled at the base of his neck, and he realized that something dramatic was occurring. He was changing, then changed.

Rob looked at the world around him—asphalt and bikers and beach grass and sand and telephone wire lined with gulls—in a stupor. He was brimming with joy and generosity. He thought of Liz and Donnie and wished them well; in this new reality he saw them not as his adversaries but as his sister and brother in Christ. His love for them and for his boys and for every living creature radiated with magnanimity.

Traffic started moving and Rob found a Christian station on the radio. He sang along to the worship songs. He contemplated which church he might like to attend back at home and what sort of good women he might meet there. He thought how happy it would make his parents to learn that he had found the Lord—he would call them as soon as he got home. This news would almost certainly make his father want to talk to him again. He tried to remember and recite aloud scripture he had memorized as a child. He felt extremely certain of Jesus and himself.

But the trouble was that the drive home was too long. Rob had too many hours alone in the car, and the feeling of conversion began to fade about halfway through, just outside of Baltimore. Had he gotten home within the hour, Rob was sure he could have maintained the feeling, but instead the long hours turned to idle thoughts and fast food. Boredom, skepticism, pessimism crept in. And by the time he was back at home, he had talked himself out of the Christian faith.

Rob went to bed exhausted, empty, and bereft.

The next day and over the course of the next week, Rob did all sorts of things in the interest of transformation. He fasted for two days. He started a new vitamin regimen. He tried (and failed) to locate and get in contact with his high school girlfriend. He pierced his ear. He took scalding-hot baths and ice-cold showers. He listened to jazz music with his eyes closed. He bought many books. He thought about his parents' lives. He reorganized his closet. He stared at old photographs. He made requests and demands of the universe. He focused on his breath. And although each of these measures held the promise of truth and was undertaken with hope and determination and even something that resembled courage, even still, after all of this, the heart that thrashed in his chest would not change—that stubborn little beast, the god of him, it would not change.

JUNE 1995

PART 3

JANET SHOWED UP TO CORINNE'S HOUSE HALF AN HOUR early, and Corinne took ages to recover from the interruption to her nap—she kept yawning to hammer this point home.

The two of them sat together at the kitchen table and got organized: a packet of pens and thank-you cards in front of Corinne, stamps and stickers and envelopes and address book before Janet. Corinne got to work on the notes while Janet started to address envelopes.

They had not made much progress before Janet's pen broke and splurted out a pool of blue ink. Most of the mess was on her fingers and the paper and tabletop before her, but a few droplets made their way onto her pink shirt. "Dammit," she muttered.

Corinne said, "That'll come out."

"No way. It's already soaked in. Ruined."

"You can use my hair spray on it, that's supposed to be the best thing." Corinne gazed at the envelope her mother had been working on, then bent to look closer. "Are you addressing one to yourself?"

"I got you a gift, didn't I? Not to mention hosting. The food. Et cetera. But I guess I shouldn't expect a formal thank you from my daughter. Or an informal one."

"I've thanked you ten times at the very least for hosting and the bassinet."

"There was also that bottle warmer I found on discount months ago. The maternity clothing I drove all the way to Kristy's house to pick up for you. And twice I picked up stuff to help with your nausea. Doesn't matter."

"Your memory is incredible," Corinne said. "A gift to us all." Corinne was always marveling about her mother's memory. She rose from the table. "I'll be right back with the hair spray."

"It will not work," Janet said. "For God's sake, Corinne, can you just let a thing be? Just leave me alone."

Corinne stared at her mother.

"Leave me alone," Janet repeated.

Corinne sat back down and they continued to work on the cards in silence.

When Corinne passed her mother a card that opened with *Dear Mom (Janet)* . . . Janet crumpled it up without reading it.

Corinne shook her head in disbelief. "Impossible."

"Plenty of people love me," Janet said.

When all the envelopes were addressed, Janet drummed her blue fingertips on the table while she waited for Corinne to finish the notes. It was a shame about this pink shirt, but it would be helpful for Corinne to recall that this activity had involved a sacrifice on Janet's part. That made the whole ordeal feel like a win.

And what did Janet know about ink stains? Corinne had wanted to know. Plenty, as it turned out.

Janet's aunt Corinne was very poor and could barely provide for herself and young Janet when she took her in. She did her best. But Janet had only one skirt, which she wore every day. Some of the kids at her school noticed this and gave her a hard time. One day Janet said softly to the ringleader of the teasing, a cruel boy who went by Buck, in the hopes that this would put an end to it: "I don't wear the same skirt every day; I have five or six of the same exact one."

"Oh, yeah?" Buck whipped a pen out of his backpack and moved quick as a snake to mark a long dark line on the thigh of Janet's skirt. "We'll see tomorrow."

Back at her aunt Corinne's house, Janet had tried everything to get the pen mark out: hand soap, dish soap, shampoo, rubbing alcohol. Aunt Corinne did not know anything about Buck, but in an effort to help her niece salvage the garment, she offered hair spray, which she'd heard was effective on ink. But still the stain did not lift. So Janet borrowed one of her aunt Corinne's skirts for school the next day, even though it was so big it had to be pinned and tucked, and it actually made matters far worse where Buck and his posse were concerned.

The point was, and what Janet could not for the life of her understand why Corinne was so unwilling to accept, that sometimes a thing was just plain ruined.

Janet looked at her watch, gathered her things, and rose from the table. "Gotta go. Your father needs me."

"What for?" Corinne asked.

"Everything," Janet said over her shoulder.

Corinne laughed in a manner that was so unexpectedly warm—affectionate, even—it caused Janet to stop at the door.

There was a fierce urge pushing up through her: the desire to confide in her daughter, perhaps even to find a friend in her. There was so much Janet wanted to tell Corinne. For example, how there were aspects of Bruce's confusion that made sense and which Janet could easily rectify—him forgetting the day of the week, for instance, or the name of a neighbor—and other changes that were so strange that Janet could not bear to address them, so they simply broke her heart again and again, like how he never closed his eyes during prayer anymore.

Her urge to share with her daughter was soon a mass so great and so tactile that it was clogging Janet's throat, making it impossible to exhale, much less voice any fearsome truths.

Janet could only breathe again when she was out of her daughter's home and free of her daughter's superpower—or perhaps it was every daughter's superpower: her ability to give and to take so much and so fast that a mother could never feel anything fully, and a mother could never feel anything safely.

JULY 1995

PART 1

TEMPERATURES ALL ACROSS THE MIDWEST WERE SOAR-
ing when Ellen's air-conditioning went out. Apparently, people
in Chicago were actually dying of the heat. Hundreds of people.
Ellen was not dead but she was in misery. The A/C had stopped
working in the middle of the night on Friday and she didn't get
any return calls from technicians on Saturday morning. She killed
some time at the library and the grocery store and took a few cool
baths. But by Saturday afternoon, with the temperature still above
one hundred and the forecast calling for a few more days of this,
she was no longer thinking straight.

Michael was not particularly handy but had occasionally
been able to diagnose and fix a mechanical problem around the
house. She dialed his number. He did not pick up. He had an answering machine, and Ellen left a message: "It's me. I know we
haven't talked in a while. My A/C's out. Any chance you could
come take a look?"

She knew she could count on a return call from Michael but didn't know when. They were not in touch frequently. He did not ever initiate contact. Still, she thought she would put on something decent just in case he came to take a look. It wouldn't be like him to show up unannounced, but just in case. After getting herself into a nice outfit, Ellen went to the freezer, dumped the fresh cubed ice into another container, and refilled the trays. She guzzled grape juice straight from the jug. She paced the house, stood in front of the fan, and ran an ice cube over her brow. Eventually she decided to pursue options other than Michael, because she was tired of waiting for him. She considered which of her friends' husbands was the most likely to know a thing about an A/C unit. Dare she interrupt somebody's weekend for this? She hated to look like a sad sack.

Then she had the idea to call Gary. They had a monthly dinner date nowadays. It was a regular thing, the first Friday of the month; she picked the place, he picked up the tab. It was something to look forward to. Gary seemed to have his drinking under control, and now that the pressure was off for a romance she got a bang out of him—there was usually a lot of laughing. She always ordered dessert. Sometimes even coffee or tea after that.

There was nothing to suggest that Gary was any more of a handyman than Michael, but Ellen thought it was worth a shot. For some reason she felt less embarrassed calling him for help than anyone else who came to mind.

Gary answered after a few rings. He sounded surprised and happy to hear from Ellen mid-month like this. He said, "Something happen? Did your granddaughter come a month early?"

"No, not yet," she said, impressed that Gary remembered

Corinne's approximate due date and the baby's sex. "It's my air-conditioning. It's broken. I'm dying."

"I bet," Gary said. "I haven't left the house since Thursday. When did it go out?"

"Last night. I called every repairman I could find in the phone book this morning, and of course nobody's picking up on the weekend. What do you know about air-conditioning?"

"Not a thing," Gary said.

"Shoot," Ellen said. "Do you have a fan I could borrow? Mine's just barely pushing anything through. Do you have one of those big square ones that sits on the floor? I don't really want to buy a new one just for a couple days."

"I don't own one of those. I have one of the stand-up kind that oscillates. It works all right but it makes a racket. I also have a small one that you could have on your bedside table right next to your face. That one puts a lot of air through for a little guy."

"Maybe I could borrow them if your air-conditioning is doing the trick for you."

"Sure thing. You want me to drive them over? I don't have anything going on."

"No, no, I'll come to you. What's your address?"

Ellen had never been to Gary's house. She knew from the location that it would be nice, situated in a cul-de-sac near the hospital, but it was far more charming than she imagined. It was a small, blue, Cape Cod–style home with white trim and sage-green shutters. Several towering maples provided shade. A large mulch bed bursting with orange zinnias and marigolds lined the front of the home.

Did Gary tend these flowers or pay someone else to? What a surprise, either way.

He answered the door promptly. He was not holding a fan. She said, "Your house is very nice." She peered over his shoulder. "And very clean."

Gary laughed. "Are you surprised?"

"A little."

"Fans are all set to go. But I was wondering if I could entice you to have a lemonade with me before you head home."

He was wearing a blue polo shirt and khaki shorts and ankle socks. She had never seen his legs before. They were incomprehensibly pale.

"It does feel wonderful in here," Ellen said.

He walked her down a hall and into the kitchen, where he pulled out a chair. He said, "It's more like a lemon slushy, actually, I didn't get the concentrate thawed." He stirred a pitcher with a wooden spoon, then poured chunky yellow lemonade into two cups.

Ellen sipped. "My word, that is refreshing." She drank some more and pressed the frozen bits to the roof of her mouth with her tongue to crush and melt them. "I went to the library this morning just to sit for a while to escape the heat of my house. Then I walked around the grocery store for an hour, for two items."

Gary said, "You're welcome to stay as long as you like. In fact, you can stay the night if you want. I thought about offering that when you called, but I didn't want to come off weird. But I can set up the guest bedroom for you. It has its own bathroom."

"That's quite an offer," Ellen said. She thought about this. It did seem a little weird. But maybe not. They were good friends. She could pack a bag like she was going to a hotel. She wondered if there was a TV in the guest bedroom. She said, "I would need to go home to let Rocky out right before bed. Well and now that I'm thinking about it, I'd worry with the heat. In case he knocked over his water dish or something. I'd worry too much about Rocky. But thank you for the offer."

"You could bring Rocky over here," Gary pointed out.

"Oh, I wouldn't dare. Your house is so clean."

"Don't be ridiculous," Gary said. "If you're trying to be polite and using Rocky as your excuse, we'll leave it at that. But if you're actually worried about him crapping on my carpet, get over it, that's no big deal."

"I don't know," Ellen said again. She gazed around the kitchen. "Do you clean yourself or pay someone? I'm sorry, that's so rude. I'm just curious."

"Mostly I do it myself, but I pay a gal to come once every few months because there are places I can't do easily myself. The baseboards, for example. Kills my back. Are you hungry?"

"I could eat," Ellen said.

"I've got calzones in the big freezer downstairs. I know you like that kind of thing."

When Gary left the kitchen to go to his basement freezer, Ellen got up to poke around the room.

A calendar hung beneath the phone mounted to the wall. The calendar had almost nothing on it. Her eyes traveled to the first Friday of this month, where in neat printing it said *Ellen*, followed by an exclamation point. This exclamation point startled her and she looked away.

Gary returned to the kitchen. "You got time to wait for the oven to preheat? I could do microwave but they're better crisped up."

"Sure thing," Ellen said.

He set the oven to preheat, unwrapped the frozen calzones, and set them on a baking sheet.

Ellen went to the glass sliding door that looked into his backyard, then she looked into the adjoining dining room, where a large table was covered with tools and odd supplies. It was the only part of the house she'd seen so far that was untidy. "What's that?" she said.

"Oh." Gary moved to shield her view into that room. "It's a surprise."

"Why? For what?"

"For you. Well, sort of."

"Me?"

Gary glanced over his shoulder. "I guess the surprise part is ruined." He stepped aside to permit her entry. "Maybe you can help me with colors."

Ellen approached the table and looked over an array of wooden rods, scraps of sandpaper, glue, a ball of twine, some tubes of acrylic paint, brushes, pencils, pliers, scissors, and many wooden beads, some of them painted green and pink but most of them still bare. A layer of protective newspaper covered the table.

"What is it?" she said.

"An abacus." Gary positioned the pieces of wood together roughly on the table to demonstrate what the frame would look like. "For your granddaughter."

"My word!" Ellen picked up one of the painted beads and rolled it around her hand.

"I'm not very good with kids. But when my daughter was little I made her something like this and she just loved it. Now, your granddaughter won't be able to play with it for a year or two, but

I thought I'd go ahead and try to have it ready to give to her as a present for when she's born."

"I don't know what to say."

Gary pulled his reading glasses from where they hung at his collar, put them on, and stirred his finger around the beads. "Do you like green and pink? I wasn't sure about the shade of green. And I was thinking about doing a row of yellow, too, then the bottom row, all the colors, alternating. But I wasn't sure about the color for the frame. Do you think this green is all right? Is it tacky?"

"It's perfect. This is so special."

"Really?" Gary straightened his glasses.

The oven beeped and Ellen followed him into the kitchen, where he put the calzones in.

They sat back down at the kitchen table.

Gary said, "You must've struck out left and right to make it all the way down to me, on your list of people to call in a crisis."

"Actually," Ellen said, "You were number two. I called my ex first. He didn't pick up." She flicked a crumb from her arm. "Are you in touch with your ex? You haven't mentioned her in a while."

"She's still with the excavator. I assume they're together for the long haul. So we don't speak often, but it's not hostile."

Ellen said, "You seem a lot less hostile these days, in general. It's none of my business, but I notice you don't order alcohol anymore."

"That's part of it," Gary rose to peer into the oven, then he got plates and silverware and set the table. "I really have to credit this support group I'm in. We meet at the Lutheran church. The paper ran a little notice advertising the group a while back and I thought, what the hell. And I've been going regularly ever since."

"AA?"

Gary shook his head. "It's a support group for divorced men. Alcohol was obviously part of the issue for me too when it came to coping, but this group has helped with the big picture."

"That's wonderful," Ellen said.

"It's pathetic is what it is. Bunch of losers sitting around talking about how lonely they are."

She laughed. "You talk about your divorces and stuff?"

"Some guys talk about their divorces. Exes. Stuff they regret. Or stuff they're still mad about. Some talk about their children. Work. Stress. Depression. Booze. Mostly we just listen to one another. There's not much in the way of advice."

"Maybe I should be in something like that."

"You don't seem hung up on anything to me," Gary said.

"It might be a nice experience."

"Is your ex still with the hairdresser?"

"What? Oh, that. I made that up," Ellen said. "It wasn't about another woman, that I know of. I just didn't know how else to describe what had happened. The hairdresser seemed like a good story. The truth is that I still don't know why he left me."

Gary regarded her. "Really? He never gave you a reason?"

Ellen shook her head. "He said 'drifted away.' Or 'apart.' I figured, after almost forty years, surely there was more to it. Surely there was another woman. He insisted not. Just the drifting."

"That sounds like a truly unique kind of divorce hell."

"I spent so long trying to figure it out," Ellen said. "I was obsessed. For a while it was the only thing I thought about, day in and day out, all the things that were wrong with me. I figured if there was no woman then it had to be something bad about me, and I got determined to figure out which was the worst. Which one had put him over the edge." She fiddled with the fork on the table before her. "I think I know what it was now, though. I think I finally figured out what it was."

"What was it?"

"That I take too long to tell a story."

Gary snorted and lemonade spluttered out of his nose. "Oh my God," he said. "I'm sorry." He looked like he was trying not to laugh but he couldn't keep it in. He waved his hand in the air. "I'm sorry," he said again. He let himself go and laughed until he wheezed. He got up to grab a paper towel and blew his nose into it. He took off his glasses, wiped his eyes and nose. Then he said, "Can I kiss you?"

"What? Why?"

"Because I like you so much. And you're really hot."

"I am?" Ellen stared at him. "Really?"

"Are you kidding? Do you see how people look at us when we're out together? They must assume I'm loaded. Or, like, a decorated veteran. Or that I have a great personality. Hah!"

Ellen laughed.

Gary said, "I'm serious, you are one sexy lady."

"Really? Sexy? Okay. Wow. Really? Okay. I do not want to have sex, though."

"Heard." Gary came over and leaned down to give her a chaste, closed-lip peck. He stood back up, patted her head, and said, "There."

Ellen said, "A little more than that would be okay."

"You take the lead then."

Ellen stood up to face him and she leaned in and gave him a better, deeper kiss. His mouth was very cold and lemony. After a few seconds she was stunned to realize that something had awakened inside her and was pressing outward.

She pulled away to look at him and said in disbelief, "I changed my mind. Maybe I do want to have sex."

They moved slowly. Gary was gentle. Ellen kept laughing and apologizing for laughing, saying, "It's just, for some reason everything tickles."

When they were done they lay together on their backs and for the first time in many, many years, Ellen felt like she might be looking beautiful.

"Oh shit," Gary said. "The calzones."

They dressed and went downstairs.

Gary pulled the calzones from the oven—they were black and releasing smoke. He said, "I've got more in the freezer."

Ellen told him she was going to go home to pack a bag for the night and give Rocky a little bath before bringing him over, and they could have calzones when she came back.

Back at her house, it was a moment before Ellen noticed something was not as she expected. She listened and realized to her surprise that the air-conditioning was working. She went out back to double-check and, sure enough, the exterior unit was humming away.

She let Rocky out, then stood in the kitchen marveling at this unexpected gift. She considered the possibility that Michael had gotten her message, come and let himself in, and fixed it for her. Or maybe it was not Michael that had done her a kindness but the universe. Because under what other circumstance would she have ever found her way into Gary's home and his bed? One glancing thought of Gary and his home and his bed made her heart feel wild; between her legs she still felt open, damp, different.

She wondered if she dared go back to Gary's for the night even though the problem here was fixed. She thought she'd call Gary and tell him about the changed situation here and see if he was still keen on her returning.

Before she had dialed him though, she had an important thought: now that it was only a month until Corinne was due, the baby phone call could happen any time. She would not want to receive that news late. Of course she could call Paul now, give him Gary's number, and tell him to call there if anything should happen, but that seemed like a whole can of worms. Paul might ask questions.

While Ellen was mulling this over her phone rang.

She picked it up.

It was Michael. "I got your message," he said. "Sorry I didn't get it sooner, I was taking a nap and didn't hear the phone."

"It's okay," Ellen said. "But now it's fixed and it's working. Thank you for calling. I'm fine now. Thank you." She was stammering. She realized she was terrified that her voice alone might reveal to Michael—who had perhaps not even kissed another woman since their divorce—what she had done with Gary.

"Oh," Michael said. "Well, that's good. What was the issue?"

"The issue?"

"With the air-conditioning. I assume someone else fixed it for you?"

Ellen thought through the full story of her day, which she would of course not tell Michael: Lemon slush, calzones. The abacus. Gary's pale legs. Gary's way of touching her. Michael was the

only other sexual partner Ellen had ever had in her life. She had
not even really known there were other ways to do it—ways that
made everything feel loose inside of her instead of tight. She truly
didn't know what to make of any of this. She wondered, If she told
Michael the story from today, would he tell her the story of why
he left her? This was the problem with stories: there was always so
much more to tell than a person needed, or wanted, to know.

PART 2

THEY WERE ON DAY FIVE OF THE WORST HEAT WAVE
Bruce had ever experienced. Janet was off to the pool with Corinne
for the afternoon, and she had said they would probably shop for
baby stuff and do ice cream, too. Bruce was sipping a Pepsi in the
La-Z-Boy and trying to get comfortable enough for a nap, when
he heard a noise. It was so faint he almost mistook it for his own
breath. It was not that, although it did resemble breath in its
cadence—wheezy and rhythmic.

Bruce looked around the room. TV, off. Radio, off. Door,
closed. Fan, whirring and trembling as it oscillated, producing a
sound but not *the* sound.

Bruce closed his eyes and tried to ignore it, but there was
something in the sound that disturbed him, so he got out of the
chair to investigate. Once he was standing it was clear the noise
was coming from outside. Bruce peered out of the side window.
Raymond, the next-door neighbor, a widower, was a few years

older than Bruce, and it struck Bruce that Raymond could be in some kind of trouble. A thick tree line obstructed a clear view of Raymond's lawn from this window, so Bruce decided he'd better venture out.

At the door, the heat hit Bruce solidly and at once, as if a quilt that had spent hours in the oven was thrown over him.

The grass was gray and dead.

The sun screamed into his eyes.

From here Bruce could see that Raymond's car was gone, which made sense; Raymond was retired but volunteered at the Salvation Army every Saturday. So then there was almost no chance that Raymond was producing the sound. Could it be an appliance of some kind? Bruce wondered. Raymond's air-conditioning unit struggling? Something with the plumbing, creating an odd pressure and release of air? Bruce stilled himself for a moment to listen once again. The sound was louder now. Bruce looked left and right. The sound faltered and petered out for a moment, then started in again, at a higher pitch and a quicker tempo. There was life in it, he realized, and pain.

Bruce walked in the direction of Raymond's backyard. He passed beneath the sycamore and squeezed between the forsythias. Bruce and Raymond were friendly enough that he had no trepidation at crossing the property line. Raymond was a gentle man who watered plants and collected mail for Bruce and Janet when they vacationed. Sometimes he brought fresh muffins.

In the middle of Raymond's lawn, Bruce's eye caught on the glint of metal. In the glaring sun it was hard to look at the object directly.

It was a large cage trap, the right size to hold a rabbit or a groundhog. But it held neither of those—inside the trap was a cat.

Understanding slowly reached Bruce as he recalled a recent conversation.

Raymond had become an avid birder since the death of his beloved wife several years ago. He had installed feeders and houses and done everything he could to make his plot hospitable to the local bird population. A week ago when Bruce was on the porch and Raymond was returning from a walk, Raymond had approached to ask Bruce if he'd had any run-ins with a big tomcat; Bruce had not. Raymond reported that it seemed to be a stray based on its bedraggled appearance and fear of humans. He said the cat had killed several birds on his property. Raymond told Bruce he had tried various tactics to keep the cat away but the cat kept coming back, having identified his property as fertile hunting ground.

Raymond's distress at the dead birds and the possibility of more was apparent. He looked to be on the brink of tears. He asked if Bruce had any advice.

Before Bruce could say anything, Janet, who had joined him on the porch and was listening in, said, "Just shoot the danged thing for all I care."

"I don't have a shotgun," Raymond said. "And you know I'm more of a conscientious objector, myself."

"That's right," Janet said. "One of those."

Now that Bruce had recovered this memory and understood what lay before him, he had no clue what a right-minded person might do about it.

So often these days, Bruce toiled over simple matters. He had never been a decisive man, but nowadays even his strongest convictions wobbled like Jell-O. He relied on Janet for virtually all information relating to himself, from personal beliefs to how he took his coffee.

Bruce stared into the trap. The cat was on its side and it looked wet. Its golden eyes were wild and sad.

It spotted Bruce and opened its mouth meekly to release a high and hoarse moan, then it blinked slowly.

It was panting. It was, Bruce realized, dying from the heat.

Bruce approached. The cat lifted its chin and looked directly at Bruce's eyes, something no cat had ever done before.

Bruce walked closer and said, "Good kitty. Poor kitty. Let's get you out of this heat, poor thing."

Bruce picked up the cage by its top handle and hauled it over to his house. He felt the weight of the trap shift as the cat slid limply to one end.

Inside the house, the cat pissed right away. Some of it splashed hotly onto Bruce's bare calf and lots more onto the carpet.

Janet was going to flip. She hated the smell of a cat.

Bruce thought. Water. He retrieved a dish and figured out how to maneuver one end of the trap open just enough to wedge the dish in without permitting the cat to escape, not that the cat had the wherewithal to do so. The cat eyed the water listlessly then seemed to wake to the possibility of survival, and it raised its head enough to dip its tongue into the water, then it lapped slowly.

Bruce blew on its face to cool it down and said, with a feeling of competence, "Good kitty."

He moved the floor fan so it was right next to the trap and the cat could get more cooling air. After a few minutes and more water the cat seemed better, then much better, then so good it got mad. It hissed at Bruce and clawed violently at the side of the cage.

Bruce wondered, What next? He didn't dare let the thing out of the cage lest it rip the place to shreds and continue to piss. And it didn't make sense to release it outside, where it would surely return to Raymond's lawn to commence the killing.

He wondered where Raymond was planning to take the cat and thought, Who on earth are the people to take care of such things? A city service? That seemed right. But for the life of him Bruce couldn't recall what the service would be called or how to look it up in the phone book. Not a zoo. Not a veterinary office. A person didn't call 9-1-1 for such a thing. Where was the phone book anyhow?

He thought, *I'll call Corinne.* She was an animal lover, she'd know what to do.

Corinne didn't pick up though; it was Paul.

Paul said, "She's at the pool. With Janet, I thought."

"Oh, duh," Bruce said. "You're right. I just forgot."

"What's up?"

"I've got myself in a pickle here."

"Oh yeah?"

"My neighbor trapped a cat. He's gone to his volunteer shift and usually doesn't get back till four or five. The thing was about to croak in the heat out there, so I brought it in. Revived it. It pissed all over the floor."

"Oh brother. Janet hates cats, doesn't she?"

"I'll clean that up, that's not why I called. I called, well, I forgot about Corinne being out. I was going to get her advice. I'm at a loss for what to do with this thing. I don't know what Raymond had planned. What do you do with a stray? Dump it in the woods? It's mean as hell. Apparently it hunts birds. What would you do?"

"Take it to the humane society. They'll take it in and handle it."

"Of course," Bruce said, with relief. "Humane society. See?

Silly old me. I couldn't think of the name for that place. Do you know where it's located?"

"Why don't you let me come pick it up and take it?" Paul said. "You've probably got your hands full, getting the carpet cleaned up before Janet gets home."

"That's true. But I hate to rope you in on this," Bruce said.

"I don't have anything going on. I'll leave right away, be there in ten."

Paul showed up with his car all ready for the task—the back seat emptied and old towels laid out across the upholstery.

Hours later when Janet had still not yet returned, Bruce saw Raymond's car pulling in.

He went out the front door to deliver the good news.

Raymond parked and got out. Bruce waved and walked toward him. "Got your cat."

"Come again?" Raymond cupped his hand at his ear.

"Heard the thing out there a couple hours ago," Bruce said. "Struggling in the heat. Must've caught him this morning, after you left."

"What? Oh, oh. Last night actually."

"Huh?"

"He was rattling around in the trap this morning when I got up."

"Oh." Bruce frowned. "But . . ."

"With the heat and all, I figured I'd just let nature run its course." Raymond was holding a few pieces of mail and looking through them absently.

"Oh," Bruce said again.

Confusion crashed into Bruce and dragged him under like a

wave as he attempted to understand the course of nature. He tried
to make sure his face did not reveal the fact that suddenly he understood nothing, most especially cruelty.

Individual matters small and large eluded Bruce all the time,
but he was always able to seize on to something that would orient
him. So he was wrong about what he'd eaten for breakfast, but he
was right about what they'd discussed having for dinner. He was
wrong about what year it was now, but he was right about what year
he was born. In this moment though, every single thing about existence was impenetrable and wrong. He grappled for something
familiar, or at least sensible, and found nothing.

Raymond picked his nose, then walked away, into his own
home. Bruce did not move.

The world had gone completely upside down. Bruce's mind
was a damp, rotten log, teeming with worms. He could not understand cats or death or faces or time. The sun was not round, but
it was everywhere; it was the entire sky. Where was God today?
Bruce couldn't understand who was in charge here. No really, he
thought in a sheer panic, who is in charge?

JULY 1995

PART 3

PAUL HAD ARRANGED HIS WORKDAY SO THAT HE COULD take Corinne to her appointment. She had done most of these by herself but asked Paul to join today because she was getting very close and disliked driving alone. She said today's appointment ought to be quick—they would take her weight and vitals and check the baby's heart rate; no ultrasound unless something seemed off.

When they arrived at the OB's office, Corinne checked in with the elderly receptionist, Lou, who had a bouncy blond ponytail that appeared to basically be taped to her head. Paul tried not to stare but then thought that surely such a thing was meant to be looked at.

Paul and Corinne took a seat in the small, dark waiting room. Corinne leaned back, rubbed her belly, and sighed. Her exhale sounded thin, like there was barely enough room to pass even this small bit of air through her body.

She said, "You don't have to come back."

"You sure?"

She nodded toward Paul's briefcase which rested at his feet. "I know you have work."

Paul was grateful. He did have work. And he always felt self-conscious around the staff here. He didn't know what sorts of things were discussed—if, for example, Corinne talked about their sex life. He wondered if they knew more than he did. Aside from food, it was so hard to guess what Corinne wanted these days.

Paul was the only man in the waiting room. There were four women besides Corinne. Two were visibly pregnant, the third looked too old, and the fourth too young.

Corinne picked up a *Cosmopolitan* magazine but had not even opened it when a nurse appeared at the side door to call her back.

Paul reached into his briefcase and withdrew his paperwork. He looked at the most recent reports he had printed out just before leaving the office and reviewed the information he would present at the management meeting tomorrow.

Several more women arrived and checked in with Lou.

One of the visibly pregnant ones was called back by a nurse, and Paul did not give this any attention until she paused at the front desk to say something to Lou.

"What, honey?" Lou said, tapping her own ear.

The patient repeated herself, this time loudly enough for Paul to hear: "If a man comes here saying he's with me and he wants to come back, do not let him."

Lou's eyebrows rose, then gathered into a knot. "Do I need to get the cops on the horn?"

Paul snuck a peek at the patient. She looked to be about thirty, dark hair piled high on her head. She wore an engagement ring with a nice big diamond on it, much bigger than the one Paul had proposed to Corinne with.

"I don't think he'll force his way in," the patient said. "That wouldn't be like him. I'm just saying, just in case."

"Well, for pity's sake. Warn them in the back, too. The nurses."

Paul exchanged nervous eye contact with another woman in the waiting room after the patient disappeared with the nurse; then he watched as Lou got up from her desk.

She returned and took a phone call.

Momentarily, jingle bells against the door announced the arrival of someone new but it was not any kind of man, just another pregnant woman. Nevertheless Paul was too jumpy and distracted to continue his work, so he put the reports back in his briefcase and zipped it shut.

On high alert, Paul's eyes traveled speedily through the room, identifying three doors—outdoor entry, single-stall public restroom, passage back into the offices—a single floor-to-ceiling window to the outside, and the large plexiglass window that Lou sat behind. A large fake tree, its greenery grayed with a layer of dust, obscured Paul's view of the parking lot through the window; he would not see a newcomer until they were in.

He was the only man in this space and possibly the only man in the building; Corinne's OB was a woman, as were all of the nurses and midwives and ultrasound technicians that Paul had ever encountered here.

Paul pictured a huge, bearded man wearing steel-toed boots. Then he pictured a small but muscular man with oily hair and gold teeth. He pictured a man in a suit with a calm demeanor but terrible eyes. He pictured different types of holsters for different types of weapons.

He pictured himself standing and speaking. Shouting. Leaping. Lunging?

He contemplated the logistics of a citizen's arrest and the legality of a self-defense claim if violence should be required.

Paul gazed around the room and wondered if all of these vulnerable women and their Birdies knew what he was capable of, willing and prepared to do.

He startled once again to the sound of a door opening, but it was not the exterior door; a nurse had appeared at the entry leading back to the offices. She glanced furtively around the room, her eyes resting on Paul, before calling for a patient who rose and followed.

Moments later a different nurse appeared at this door to peer into the waiting room, but she did not call a name.

When this happened again moments later, Paul attempted meaningful eye contact with the nurse at the door.

Several more patients arrived but no men.

Eventually, the woman who had issued the initial warning reappeared in the waiting room. She used the public restroom, then exited the building unceremoniously.

Shortly after, Corinne came too. She was carrying a manila folder and sucking on a mint.

In the car, Corinne said, "Tell me about this bad guy I overheard the nurses talking about."

Paul pulled out of the parking lot. The asphalt appeared to quiver in the heat. "There was a patient who said a bad guy might be coming, trying to muscle his way into her appointment. He never showed up though."

They approached an intersection where, in the median, a thin man was slumped on a folding chair and holding a handwritten sign that read, *Vietnam Vet. Need $. God bless.*

Paul reached into the center console for a handful of quarters, but before he could lower his window, Corinne said, "He looks like he's about nineteen years old. I don't think Vietnam was the problem and I don't think money's the solution."

Paul knew she was right, but it was so hot out.

The light turned green and Paul accelerated through the intersection.

"Anyway," Corinne chomped noisily into her mint. "The nurses definitely said the bad guy was there. They were all nervous about it."

"Lou probably told them wrong. I was the only guy there the whole time."

"Oh my God," Corinne said, with a laugh. "Then they must have thought it was you. They were all taking turns going out to peek so they could make a description to cops if they had to. That's so funny!" She opened the manila folder on her thighs. "Were you nervous, waiting all that time for the bad guy to show up?"

Paul adjusted his sunglasses. "I was ready to . . . doesn't matter."

"Ready to spring into action?" Corinne laughed again and insisted, "It *is* funny."

Paul nodded at the folder. "What's that?"

She leafed through a few sheets. "Labor indications. Directions to the hospital. Numbers to call. What to pack. Other random stuff. Oh look, there's even a sheet for you." She pulled this one out and glanced over it. "How to install a standard car seat. Make sure we have plenty of gas in the car. Think about what snacks we might want and have them ready in advance." She paused. "I imagine I'd be happy about a bag of Bugles and some Dots." She flipped the paper to take a look at the back, which was empty. "That's it. Think you can handle all that?"

Paul had no idea what he could handle.

The sun was colossal, casting a harsh metallic film over everything in sight. Time felt slow and pitiless. Questions oozed through Paul's mind.

Obviously a bag of Bugles, some Dots, and a full tank of gas were not enough. So, then, was love enough to make a father out of a man? Or a good man out of a bad one?

Paul wanted to turn around and go back, to give that guy in the median all of the money he had on him even if it was going to go straight to drugs or booze, not because it was the right or good thing to do but because he longed for a straightforward exchange: a desire, met.

They passed Wendy's, Rite Aid, a Chevron station, a vacant brick building, Jo-Ann Fabrics, and Crunch Fitness, where a bony old man wearing a sleeveless shirt and khaki pants was entering. Paul thought he really ought to join a gym—he went for a run every morning but had no upper-body strength. He didn't imagine Corinne would have patience for him to go in and inquire about a new membership now, so he drove on. Paul's thoughts were hurtling about senselessly now, flailing at any stray notion to distract himself from the fact that he could not get his father's face out of his head and he could not wipe his father's face off of his own.

Then Paul had another urge. He'd heard it said that becoming a father grounded you. He realized that more than anything this was what he wanted: to be shoved into a hole in the ground so tightly that he could not move a single muscle, much less try, or fail, to be any kind of man.

AUGUST 1995

PART 1

AFTER SEVERAL HOURS OF HARD LABOR THE NURSE said it was time to check Corinne's progress, meaning the dilation of her cervix, which would need to reach ten centimeters for the baby to pass through.

Corinne gasped to Paul, "I bet I'm at nine."

Paul said, "I bet you're right."

The nurse withdrew her gloved hand and announced, "You are at one and a half."

AUGUST 1995

PART 2

AFTER ALL OF THAT WAS DONE WITH, WELL, WHAT could be said of holding her child for the first time? She felt like the sun had slammed into her. In one instant, she became skinless and new and known. Yesterday and tomorrow broke into separate pieces and shot out apart from one another. What could ever be said of a moment that happened in no language, but in every language?

AUGUST 1995

PART 3

JANET STARED AT THE DRY-ERASE BOARD OUTSIDE OF Corinne's room in the recovery wing of the hospital before entering. In sloped, bulbous cursive that looked like it belonged to some teenybopper, with a heart over the *i* and everything, it read, *Welcome, baby Olivia Grace!*

Janet had braced herself for this sort of news, but seeing it in some stranger's writing was somehow even worse than learning directly from her daughter that they had not chosen a family name. Now Janet's disappointment was clanging as loud as a damn bell and she squeezed Bruce's hand so hard he said, "Ouchie."

They entered the room. Paul was not around. Corinne was asleep in the reclining chair, and the tiny baby, wrapped in a white swaddle and wearing a pink cotton cap, was cradled against her chest.

Janet said, "We're here," to wake her daughter.

Corinne's hair was greasy. Her eyes fluttered open and traveled down to the baby in her arms before she seemed to register her visitors. Finally Corinne looked up and around the room and she smiled at her parents.

Bruce moved closer and peered down at the baby with tenderness and emotion and he whispered, "Hello!"

Corinne said at full volume, "You don't have to tiptoe around. She sleeps through anything. She barely cries at all." Corinne used a button to raise her position in the chair. "Her name is Olivia Grace."

"I saw," Janet said.

Corinne shifted around. She kissed Olivia's nose and whispered to her like they were already best friends. She straightened the tiny hat across her brow. Olivia stirred but did not open her eyes. She looked so peaceful. In spite of the name business, Janet couldn't help feeling moved by her granddaughter's beauty.

Corinne said to Janet, "Here," and gestured with her chin for her mother to approach and take the sleeping baby.

Terror hissed through Janet. What if her granddaughter, who apparently "barely cried at all" cried at the sight of Janet's face or the sound of her voice or the feeling of her arms? Corinne would probably think that was funny—she'd bring it up years from now. Janet recalled now that when she first met her grandsons, Rob's boys, they were both already screaming when they got passed her way, so that was no real challenge. Janet had much preferred that scenario. Being passed a happily sleeping baby who *barely cried* was a different matter entirely. There was really only one direction for it to go: downhill. This felt like a trap. So Janet kept her distance and said, "Oh, I can't. Couldn't risk it. I'm just getting over a little cold."

"That's okay," Corinne said. "Paul's got the sniffles, too. He's scoping out the cafeteria right now, he'll be back any minute. Anyway, just wash your hands really well, they say. There's the sink."

Janet felt out of control, addled and confused by conflicting impulses. She said, "I shouldn't."

"It's really okay," Corinne insisted. "If it was mild and you're getting over it, I'm sure you're not contagious anymore. You can hold her."

"No." Janet took a step back. "It wasn't that mild. I had a fever and everything. I still might, actually." She glanced at Bruce, hoping she could trust him not to question or refute this information.

Corinne regarded her mother. "You have a fever?" She instinctively clutched Olivia tighter to her own chest. "That's not good," she said in a new tone that chafed Janet. Janet had the unpleasant realization that she was probably going to hear a whole lot more of this tone from Corinne in the years to come.

Corinne continued, "That's not good for a newborn to be exposed to something like that. Why didn't you say so on the phone, Mom? I would've told you not to come at all if I knew you had a fever."

Janet was furious at herself for getting backed into this stupid corner. She said, "Well it's not that bad. It's ninety-nine instead of ninety-eight or whatever it's supposed to be. Right on the border. Might not be anything. I'm just being careful. For pity's sake, Corinne, you sure know how to make your mother feel like crap."

"Sorry," Corinne said. Apparently too weary to pursue an argument, she turned to her father instead. "Would you like to hold her, at least?"

Bruce looked at Janet like he needed her permission. Janet sighed. "Make sure you wash your hands first. In case you're coming down with it, too."

While Bruce stood at the sink with his back turned, Paul entered the room.

Corinne said to Paul, "Mom's being weird."

Janet said, "You're so mean to me."

Corinne said, "You've been counting down the days since you first found out. Begging to be our first phone call when she came. Now you're acting like you've got about as much interest in your new granddaughter as in a rotten potato."

Janet felt a swarm of bees let loose inside of her. She had to close her eyes and her mouth.

Of course it was not that Janet was not interested in her new granddaughter. It was the exact opposite of that, actually. And the trouble was that for Janet, wanting things too much had proven so dangerous throughout her life that it always seemed to send her mouth flapping off in the wrong direction.

When the buzzing in her head subsided and she opened her eyes, Bruce had rolled up his sleeves and was drying his hands.

Janet thought hopefully that Olivia would wake and start crying for Bruce, and then maybe she would get her chance when the stakes were nice and low.

How could anyone ever understand the many calculations that ran through Janet's mind in scenarios such as these? It was no wonder she had always excelled at math.

Bruce said, "I'm ready."

Janet turned to Paul and said, "I'm not being weird, I'm just being cautious. Apparently Corinne has no idea what that's like."

AUGUST 1995

PART 4

CORINNE WAS STILL HAVING SOME RECOVERY ISSUES A couple weeks after delivery, so she called the OB's office. They recommended various over-the-counter products to ease her discomfort. She knew she could ask Paul or her mother to pick them up but decided instead that it was time to venture out for her first errand alone with the baby. She looked at the thermometer outside the kitchen window—already eighty degrees. Better get going soon; it was only going to get hotter. As she began to ready herself for a trip out though, she quickly found herself daunted by both logistics and the possibility of encountering someone she knew.

Olivia was no longer the easygoing baby she had been in the earliest days following her delivery; now she would sleep only if she was being held by Corinne, and if she was not sleeping or nursing, she was screaming. This scenario would not allow for a shower, so with Olivia cradled in her elbow, Corinne did her best to cleanse herself with a washcloth, one foot hooked on the bathroom counter, and the little rinsing bottle the hospital had sent home with her. She applied fresh deodorant to dirty armpits. She applied water, then soap, then water one-handedly to her face. She dressed in cotton shorts and a lightweight button-down top. She gripped half of her hair with a clip on the crown of her head.

Olivia cried and Corinne sat in the La-Z-Boy to nurse her. The oxytocin hit as sudden as a slap; the instant Olivia latched and drew her first swallow, Corinne felt sleepy and dizzy and happy and hungry and satisfied, and loved. She stroked Olivia's head and sang softly to her. Milk pooled down her side and went from warm to cool on her skin. Olivia's little head bobbed rhythmically. Corinne looked at Olivia's ear and into it. Olivia drifted to sleep. Corinne felt overwhelmed with gratitude and goodness and she lost time for a while.

Olivia woke, and before Corinne even stood up, Olivia released some wet-sounding gas, then more. The diaper did not contain the mess, which soaked through Olivia's onesie, through Corinne's shorts, through Corinne's underwear, to her own skin. Corinne changed Olivia's diaper and outfit, then her own. She started a load of laundry. She put diapers, wipes, a backup onesie, and three pacifiers in her bag. She went to the kitchen and ate handfuls of chipped ham. The thermometer out the kitchen window now read eighty-seven. She looked at the clock and thought, Good God. An hour and a half ago she had imagined it might take ten minutes— at most fifteen—to get herself out the door.

Olivia fell asleep in the car seat on the drive to Safeway and was still sleeping deeply even after Corinne parked the car and got out, so instead of rousing her to transfer her to the carrier sling,

Corinne unhooked the whole car seat and carried it on her elbow like a gigantic purse bonking into her hip bone with each step.

She entered the store and was pleased to find that the car seat fit neatly into the base of a shopping cart.

Corinne pushed the cart and Olivia slept through the glare of fluorescent lights overhead, an intercom announcement, and a wheel of the cart catching on a lentil that caused the whole cart to snag and jerk.

Corinne felt so victorious at Olivia's persistent sleep and her own viability as a woman out in the world that she actually began to hope she would run into someone she knew. She thought she could amaze an acquaintance by informing them that her baby was only two weeks old and it was going so well that, yes, Corinne was already doing outings on her own.

She made a detour through produce and the bakery. She picked up a dozen glazed donuts and two chocolate eclairs, hoping this would cheer up Paul. He'd been in a funk since his father's visit several days ago. His parents' divorce obviously affected Paul, but he had refused to talk about it so many times that Corinne had stopped asking.

Olivia slept on.

In the pharmacy area Corinne located the items on her list: Vaseline, Preparation H, ibuprofen, and an ice pack.

She heard the familiar voice of the pharmacist, Sharon.

Corinne knew this voice and this name only because the woman was so memorably unpleasant.

Early in her pregnancy, Corinne's doctor had prescribed a medication for her severe nausea. When Corinne came here to pick it up, Sharon asked if she needed instruction on when and how to take it. Corinne said she did not and offered that it was for morning sickness. Sharon responded with a look so steeped in judgment that Corinne felt like she had been kicked in the chest. The look said that Corinne was a weenie, her doctor a fool. Mortified, Corinne then had to wait for a pharmacy tech to get her insurance company on the phone for some coding issue. She lingered in the area, out of Sharon's view but near enough to witness Sharon's interactions with more patrons. She was relieved to observe that Sharon addressed each with some measure of superiority and contempt: the diabetic, the asthmatic, the mother of twins with ear infections.

Today, there were no pharmacy patrons at the moment, but from what Corinne could overhear, Sharon was bitching out a young-looking pharmacy tech for the way he'd documented a transaction. Sharon wagged her finger around and used the word *unbelievable* a number of times. Corinne thought if her manager at Webb's ever spoke to her that way, she would be crying and quitting. She wondered if Sharon had children.

Corinne walked slowly in front of the pharmacy counter, hoping she was close enough that Sharon would acknowledge her as a potential customer, at which point Corinne would say, "Just browsing," and she would offer Sharon a good view into her cart where Olivia was still sleeping, a perfectly healthy baby despite the early exposure to anti-nausea medication.

But Sharon did not pay her any mind, so Corinne carried on.

In the shampoo aisle, Corinne's eyes fell on a woman nearby whom, briefly, Corinne mistook for one of the labor and delivery nurses who had assisted her. This was not that nurse—who was named Maria—but she resembled her in profile. Corinne thought,

What a shame that it was not Maria, whom Corinne would love to run into spontaneously. Of everyone involved at the hospital, Maria was the one who had been at Corinne's side for the most of it, struggling and journeying with composure and grace and gentle hands and loving words. When an hour after the birth Maria had said her shift was nearly over and she would be heading out soon, Corinne wept with gratitude and said, "I am so glad it was you."

Corinne had given Paul a really good laugh a few months earlier when she told him that some of her friends had chosen to have their mothers with them in the delivery room.

Olivia started to stir when Corinne was in the greeting card aisle. Corinne realized she had killed enough time in the store that when Olivia actually woke she would be very hungry, so Corinne decided it was time to head to the checkout aisle.

She paid. Olivia was really moving now, squirming in her seat.

Corinne exited the store and was about to head for the crosswalk, when she looked up and shared incidental eye contact with a tall man in an oversized gray suit who was entering.

"Oh," she said out loud without really meaning to. But once it had been spoken he was looking at her, so she added, "Hi, Trevor."

He blinked and squinted in the sun, then he said, "Oh, hi, sure, of course."

They had dated for a while when Corinne was just out of high school, before she met Paul. Trevor had played drums for the best band in town, usually with his shirt off. They met at a party. Every girl at that party, probably every party, wanted to be with him. He had chosen Corinne, for a while.

Trevor said, "Long time."

The sun felt like a weight on Corinne's face. She said, "You live in town, still?"

He nodded. "You too?" He gestured toward the car seat in her shopping cart. "Yours?"

Corinne used her hand to block the sun out of her eyes. She looked at Olivia, whose little mouth was moving like she was working up to a scream but hadn't quite mustered the energy to unleash it. Corinne said, "Yes, this is my daughter, Olivia."

Something was dribbling down the inside of Corinne's leg. She thought it was probably sweat, but since she was only two weeks postpartum, really it could be anything.

"Congrats," Trevor said neutrally. He was wearing a wedding band.

Corinne wondered if he had children. He didn't offer the information readily, and from her own struggle Corinne knew better than to ask.

"Still playing the drums?" she said.

"I teach lessons," he said. "If that counts. And I direct jazz band at the middle school."

Corinne was sweating everywhere. Her breasts were surging with fresh milk. She adjusted her position so that Olivia was both entirely in the shade and more directly in Trevor's view, and also so that the car seat obstructed his view of her own body. She wanted Trevor to keep looking at Olivia instead of her so that he could see and understand that this was the only thing that mattered now.

Trevor had called Corinne "Cory" because he said she "didn't look like a Corinne." Sometimes he took pictures of her when she was naked, without asking. Sometimes he held his camera and looked at her appraisingly then declined to take a photograph for reasons that he did not voice.

One morning, he sat in bed and watched her dress. She pulled her little cotton sports bra on and straightened it around her ribs. He was fiddling with his camera but not aiming it at her.

He said in a tone that was sort of teasing, "You don't really do anything with your boobs, do you?"

She looked at him. "What?"

He gestured at her chest with his camera hand. "*You* know." This sounded less like teasing.

She turned away, stunned and humiliated because she did know, and it was true, if she was right to assume that by "doing anything" he meant making her small breasts look bigger or higher or sexier for him—and his pictures—in some way, such as by wearing an expensive bra with matching underwear. It was true that she was not doing anything with her boobs except having them.

In the moment, Corinne tried to laugh backward over her shoulder even as the laughing smile she wore felt like a crack across her head.

That weekend, she tried to do something. She browsed at an upscale lingerie store in the mall, but even the cheapest bras were more than she could afford. She ended up at Fashion Bug, where she spent over an hour going back and forth between the undergarment section and the fitting rooms. She thought the attendant must think she was either a brazen and inefficient shoplifter or mentally insane. She just couldn't decide what to do. An understated bra might not count as doing something; leopard print could come off as pathetic.

Corinne couldn't remember now what she had settled on but it

must not have been right. Because although Trevor didn't officially
end things with her, at a certain point it seemed like he didn't want
to talk to her very much at parties anymore.

She wondered what had become of the pictures he took and was
consoled by the idea that because of her failure to do more, those
photographs were probably not part of any permanent collection.

Trevor was carrying a large sack from Taco Bell in one hand.

Corinne remembered the smell of the house he lived in when
they dated, where he and his roommates were trying so hard to
save on utilities that they didn't flush their pee.

A mother carrying a toddler walked past, into the store. Over
his mother's shoulder the toddler waved at Corinne then pushed
his nose up with his finger, like a pig's snout.

Trevor ran his free hand over his gleaming scalp and nodded
toward the Taco Bell bag he clutched. "Lunch for my wife. She
works in the pharmacy here. I try and catch her on break."

Well, now. *That* was something, Corinne thought.

Her mind went on a brief and wild journey.

She would have to get a much closer look at Sharon the next
time she was here.

Trevor shifted his weight. He was standing at the precise distance from the sliding door where it responded to every move he
made, sliding shut when he inched in Corinne's direction, open
when he moved away, and staying suspended partially open when
he was perfectly still. Behind him the sun reflected harshly off the

newspaper rack. He looked eager to be on his way but unsure how to politely bring an end to this interaction.

Actually, it occurred to Corinne, even more than that, he looked confused.

She gazed a little further into his face and realized with a start: "You don't know who I am."

Trevor grimaced with embarrassment. "I'm so sorry. My eyes are bad, especially in this sun. I can barely even see you."

Corinne was gobsmacked. She laughed.

He said again, "I'm so sorry," yet still did not ask her to elaborate on their shared past.

Corinne realized this was probably not his first encounter of this nature. Far from it. It was a small town, after all. She laughed again.

He said obligingly, "Remind me who you are?"

She said, "It doesn't matter."

Trevor seemed grateful to be relieved of this information. Corinne realized he had probably not actually wanted to know back when they were dating any more than he did now.

He rocked awkwardly a few times on his heels, and behind him the sliding door opened and closed and opened and closed.

He said, "Guess I'll head on in, then."

Corinne said, "Yes, you'd better." She didn't imagine Sharon would appreciate a cold taco.

They parted ways and Corinne went to her car. Olivia was starting to cry now and Corinne could feel her breasts throbbing. It was a fifteen-minute drive, twenty if they hit the lights wrong. She didn't want to wait, especially because there was no chance Olivia would settle— it would be nonstop screaming the whole way and she'd lose half of her milk to leakage, so Olivia might not

even be satisfied with what was left for her to consume by the time
they were settled and nursing back at home.

Corinne remembered she had a towel in the trunk; coverage
would be crucial since the windows would need to be cracked to
allow for a breeze. This would not be comfortable, but it would be
better than waiting.

She returned the shopping cart, placed the car seat back in the
car and refastened it, pulled Olivia out, retrieved the towel from
the trunk, and then situated herself and Olivia in the passenger
seat, reclining it a few inches to provide ample room for both of
them.

She positioned the towel over herself and unbuttoned her top.
Olivia found her way quickly, latching, sucking. Corinne's head
felt like it was floating off as hormones rippled ecstatically through
her. She had the feeling of extreme capacity. She hoped that Trevor
and Sharon had children if they wanted them.

When Olivia's pace slowed and that first whack of hormones ta-
pered off, Corinne opened her eyes and gazed toward the entrance
of the store. Heat rose, wobbling, from the asphalt. She watched
some people coming and going. Boyfriends and girlfriends and
husbands and wives and nearly all of them surely exes, too, to
someone—exes who had no clue which of the things they had said
and done would dissipate into the past as quick and harmless as a
puff of smoke in an empty room, and which would affix to another
life like a barnacle.

Corinne wondered if there was room in her heart for every
version of every person. A boyfriend who expected more, and a
nervous, sweating, band director with a bag of warm tacos for his
mean wife. A new mother feeding her child in a parking lot, and
a girl sifting doggedly through the clearance bin of Fashion Bug

undergarments, so determined to squash her entire being into a mold of someone else's design that for some time she forgot her own name, which had been given to her by her own mother, who had not known love until she was twelve years old.

SEPTEMBER 1995

CORINNE'S BROTHER, ROB, HAD RENTED OUT A CONDO on the Jersey Shore for a long weekend to celebrate his fortieth birthday with the family. These arrangements had been made shortly before Corinne became pregnant. Paul saw the prospect of vacationing with a newborn a perfectly reasonable excuse to bow out of the trip; Corinne did not. Somehow, though, three days and nights had budged along and it was now Sunday evening, with checkout at ten o'clock tomorrow morning.

For dinner they ate pizza on the balcony as Olivia slept peacefully in Corinne's arms and Rob's twins launched handfuls of crushed ice off the deck. After the meal, Janet insisted that Paul and Corinne stay seated and enjoy the fresh air while she cleaned up.

The ocean view was partially obstructed by the boardwalk and a minigolf course with rotating obstacles such as a windmill and a waving Tyrannosaurus rex wearing sunglasses. The late

September breeze was mellow and exquisite, and it carried the aroma of vanilla from the candy shop at the nearest access point of the boardwalk.

Paul looked at his wife. One of Corinne's breasts had leaked through her shirt. These days, he rarely knew what to say to her.

It was almost seven o'clock. Rob was readying his boys for bed, and their uproar could be heard on the deck.

Paul said, "I don't know how Rob does it. Two of them. One of him."

"Only a few days a month though," Corinne pointed out.

It gratified Paul to hear Corinne reference her brother's custody situation this way even though it was a sore spot with Rob, whose ex, Liz, had recently become engaged. Rob had surprisingly little to say about the man who would become the twins' stepfather, but it was clear the arrangement pained him. Nevertheless, all weekend Paul had watched his brother-in-law with envy as the twins reveled in their father's presence and Rob provided capably for them with blithe self-possession. Paul could not believe the careless way Rob tossed his sons' little bodies around. Paul still grew tense every time he touched Olivia, every time he looked at her. He feared for every organ inside her. Corinne said this tenseness might be part of the problem.

Corinne said, "Do you think my dad's hearing is worse?"

"I haven't been paying attention."

"It's definitely getting worse. Pay attention."

"Okay." Paul committed to this but was skeptical that his attention would yield any information about Bruce's hearing. If Janet was in the room—and she always was—she spoke for the both of them; this was nothing new. Perhaps Bruce was meandering on the periphery of conversation a bit more nowadays than before, but he didn't seem unhappy about it. Matter of fact, Paul thought, if it was the case that Bruce's hearing was getting worse, for all they knew, Bruce was reveling in silence.

Olivia snuffled in her sleep. Corinne shifted her position, said, "Shh, shh," and Olivia settled immediately. The smell of citrus reached them on the deck: Janet's omnipresent lemon Pledge, like a third arm.

It was dusk now, the sky shaded like a bruise. The streetlamps lining the boardwalk all flicked on at once.

Olivia squirmed again. Corinne said, "Can you hold her while I pee? Then I'll nurse and put her down."

Paul felt disappointed that the opportunity for a romantic moment with his wife had been squandered by Bruce's bad hearing. He reached for his daughter. As soon as Olivia's body met Paul's arms, her back arched and she began to howl. She broke free from her swaddle and punched the air with her fists.

Corinne didn't look back.

Rob emerged from the balcony onto the deck. "Damn, dude," he said, screwing an index finger into his ear.

Paul had taken to warning others, "Cover your ears, she hates me," when Corinne passed Olivia his way; it seemed to put people at ease if Paul had a sense of humor about it. And it was comical how predictable this had become. But after three days under constant observation by his in-laws who found Olivia's aversion to her father's touch a source of endless, baffling amusement, Paul was no longer in a joking spirit.

Paul observed, "The twins went down quick tonight."

"They're tuckered," Rob said loudly over Olivia's screams, then he nodded toward her. "Gimme."

Paul passed Olivia to her uncle as he had many times in the

last few days. Rob held the baby tight to his chest as he swayed and murmured something into her ear that sounded like rap lyrics. Instantly, Olivia settled. Paul met his daughter's dark blue-gray eyes as she peered down from Rob's shoulder. It was hard not to feel angry at her for failing to recognize her father's love or his desperation.

Fortunately, Rob was not in a mood to gloat. He just kept swaying and rapping, and Paul pretended that this outcome was perfect and not terrible.

Corinne returned to the balcony soon and took Olivia from her brother. She said, "I'll be back once she's asleep. Don't wait on me for a game if Mom's eager."

Rob followed Corinne into the house then reappeared a moment later with his handle of Jim Beam and two tumblers filled with ice. He set one of the tumblers in front of Paul and dangled the bottle above it. He said, "Don't make me beg, brother."

Paul nodded agreeably. Rob poured and they clinked. "I sure appreciate you making the trip," Rob said. Then he thumbed down toward the street, where Paul and Corinne's rusted teal Yugo was parked.

"You know . . ." Rob said, and in his head Paul thought, *You should really consider an SUV now that you've got a kid.*

Rob said, "Now that you have Olivia, you might think about an Explorer. Storage and safety."

There was something comforting, Paul thought, about knowing exactly when and how a person was going to belittle you.

Rob continued, "I know I've said so before. And I know they don't come cheap. I can get you the best deal you'll find anywhere, but I can't work magic." Rob had been top sales guy at his dealership for several years running. Or so he said. With Rob's history of lying it was impossible to know if this was true, although he did seem to have plenty of cash.

Rob swirled his whiskey around. "They need to give you a raise at the ol' jelly factory. Or is it jam? I can never remember."

Paul said, "Both."

Janet came out onto the balcony carrying several decks of cards and a white box from the candy shop. She removed the gold elastic around the box, pulled out several logs of fudge wrapped in wax paper, and speared each one with a little plastic knife. She said, "Corinne's taking a shower, and your father's on the toilet." She cut herself a sliver of fudge.

Rob said, "What's your cholesterol like these days, Mom?"

"Perfect." Janet turned to Paul. "We should talk holidays. I know it's your mother's year for Thanksgiving. What are you thinking for Christmas? I'd be glad to have your mother at our place if she feels like making the drive. Do you think she has strong feelings? She doesn't generally have strong feelings, does she? That's a nice quality."

Paul said, "I'm not sure where things stand. I'll talk to her."

Bruce came out and took a seat. He pointed to the fudge and said to Janet, "The one without nuts."

Janet sliced and passed him a few wedges.

Corinne joined soon, her hair still dripping wet. Her face was pink and clean. She reached for the fudge and Paul's eyes fell to her hands, those nimble little fingers that were so good at changing diapers and wrapping a snug swaddle, the fingers that Olivia found soothing to suck on when nursing was not an option and there was no pacifier in reach. Paul's fingers were clumsy and callused and provided only discord.

Rob slapped at a mosquito on his forearm.

Janet shuffled a deck of cards. "Rummy?"

On the pavement below, a couple had emerged from a neighboring condo in running clothes, and they steadied each other while they both did a hamstring stretch.

Corinne said to Paul, "You never got out for a run this weekend, did you?" To the others she said, "Poor Paul hasn't gone once since Olivia. He used to go at four thirty every morning, he never missed a day. Said it always set him straight."

Paul said, "I'll get back to it once we're all getting more sleep."

"Why don't you go now?" Corinne said. "You brought your shoes along and everything. And rummy goes better with four anyway."

Paul glanced around the table, at the others. The whiskey was burning in his chest, he was full from dinner, and he generally did not enjoy running any time of day other than first thing in the morning. But the idea of spending an hour by himself was so glorious he could have burst into song. He recognized this for what it was: a gift from his wife.

He didn't want to appear too eager. He lifted a shoulder. "Sure, if nobody minds."

Rob said, "I'll allow it."

Janet said, "You'll be missed."

Paul dressed quickly and took his wallet so that he could buy some little treat for Corinne.

From the sidewalk below he waved up toward the family, but no one was watching.

Once he was on the boardwalk Paul gazed at the music pier, where nicely dressed people were gathering for a show. Then he looked to the right, south, all the way down to the end of the commercial stretch, where the boardwalk narrowed and became residential, and then to the left, Wonderland, the amusement park, where the Ferris wheel was now lit up against the darkening sky and had started to rotate. Brightly colored rainbow lights zipped up and down the spokes. Since Paul didn't actually intend to do much running on this outing, a solitary ride on the Ferris wheel struck him as an intriguing alternative. He headed off in that direction.

The boardwalk was abuzz with evening activity. Teenagers with glow sticks wearing outfits still half-composed of swimwear. Toddlers in strollers. Balloon-animal artists. There were falconers stationed every few blocks to ward off the gulls, which had taken him by surprise on their first day here. Every time Rob passed a falconer he shouted, "Dream job!"

Paul passed the shop that sold hermit crabs, the funnel cake stand, the custom T-shirt shop. He passed the life-sized gorilla stationed at the entrance to the arcade, which beat its chest and screamed. He passed a pair of newlyweds—at least, they were dressed that way—sharing a bucket of caramel corn. He passed the jewelry store with a bare footprint for a logo.

At one point he found himself disconcertingly aroused by a woman walking in front of him when he realized a corner of her cotton shorts was mistakenly tucked up into her underwear on one side, exposing half of a butt cheek, which was very tanned and wrinkled. A tan like that, he thought, could only be achieved in a thong or in a booth. It was not a nice butt cheek. Her long ponytail looked like it had been dipped in oil.

Corinne's doctor had said sex would be fine six weeks after delivery. Paul had looked at the calendar upon receiving this instruction, and the date was stuck in his mind. It had come and gone over a week ago, and Corinne had made no mention. Paul wasn't going to push it. But he thought Corinne might be a little more eager, or at least more sympathetic, if she had any clue what sort of butt cheek had started to attract his attention.

Eventually Paul reached Wonderland, entered, and made his way through the noise and chaos—children screaming, running, crying, hugging, fighting, eating, cussing, laughing, laughing, laughing.

He reached the Ferris wheel and was relieved to see that the long line to board was moving quickly. The operator was a man wearing a newsboy cap. A middle-aged woman with pink streaks in her hair and a name tag that read FERN was collecting money.

Paul stepped up to the platform, where Fern held a zippered vinyl bag full of cash. Paul had his single ready and passed it her way.

She reached for it but then glanced over Paul's shoulder and said, "Oh, not by yourself, I'm afraid."

"What?"

"You can't ride alone." She returned the dollar.

"A money thing?" Paul reached for his wallet and pulled out another bill. "Gotta pack it full for every ride?"

"No, state law."

"There's a law that you're not allowed to ride alone?"

"As of last summer."

Paul said, "How come?"

"Some guy . . ." Fern whistled a slow arc descending in pitch and performed the corresponding gesture with her head.

Paul said, "Fell off?"

"You could say that. But, on purpose."

"Oh! Oh."

"Didn't happen here, but the law's statewide."

"Huh," said Paul.

"Bring a buddy next time," said Fern, "and I'll be happy to let you on."

"A buddy!" For some reason, this word and this predicament suddenly struck Paul as categorically hilarious. "A buddy!" He laughed so hard he gasped.

Fern looked at him like he was nuts.

Paul moved out of the way so that he wouldn't hold things up, then walked back out of Wonderland, cracking up the whole way.

He'd had enough commotion by the time he exited the amusement park and was now eager for the solitude of the ocean side of the walkway.

He crossed the boardwalk, dodging pedestrians and a person in a bear suit riding an adult-sized tricycle.

On the ocean side, Paul walked slowly with his eyes out to the water. It was churning tempestuously, with silver swells that thundered up the black beach. It was cold now, and a shiver wobbled up Paul's spine. He thought he should probably do a bit of running so that he was sporting a sweat by the time he got back to the condo but couldn't quite work his legs into motion—his muscles were so out of shape and stiffened by the cold. He gazed up at the sky. It was clear and packed with stars, more stars than he had ever seen in his life. Out of nowhere, Paul thought of his father and felt the usual activation of some dull, tired anger.

Michael had come to meet Olivia several days after her birth, not overlapping with Ellen, who had already been there. Paul was so annoyed by his father's tears, holding his granddaughter for the first time. Paul thought, *What a farce.*

He was already feeling sour toward his father before he noticed the hair. A long reddish one on his father's shoulder. Then Paul realized there were two. Maybe even three. Paul was both bewildered and incensed that his father would so sloppily disclose a new relationship in this way and that whoever the red-haired woman was, she'd most likely been in his father's arms this very morning. Paul couldn't believe Olivia was now the one nestled there against his father's chest, so close she could easily come into contact with the hairs. The thought of this made Paul physically ill.

He didn't confront his father in the moment, thinking he would not want his daughter to be present for that.

After his father departed that day, Paul had a rare inclination to talk with Corinne about his parents' divorce. He wanted to tell her how the divorce changed not only the future but also the past, if such a thing were possible; all of his childhood memories now existed behind a dirty curtain. He wanted to know if Corinne had an opinion about his father's ongoing refusal to admit that there was another woman in the picture, despite the evidence to the contrary: Friday night flowers and khaki pants in May; red hairs in August. He thought Corinne could offer helpful and attentive support—she was always encouraging him to open up about his feelings.

Paul watched his father pull out of the driveway, and it took him a few more minutes to work up the courage to talk. Eventually he said to Corinne in a shaking voice, "Did you see the hairs?"

Corinne barely even looked his way. "Huh?" she said. "Can you hand me that cloth?"

Paul looked at his wife pleadingly, knowing that if she saw his face she would see his pain, but her eyes never lifted to meet his.

"The burp cloth, Paul," she said impatiently, pointing to it, and then she was off to another room to skillfully perform some useful and necessary task.

Paul had stopped walking and turned back in order to look at the wheel, which was now turning. From this particular angle and mid-distance, its rotation seemed very fast; Paul was dizzy just watching. The bright colors smeared together against the glossy blackness. He couldn't believe just a few minutes ago he had thought it would be a good idea to be up there spinning among all of these stars.

The night sky was simply too big. It could turn a person upside down. It could cause a man to forget everything, to confuse one thing for another, like up for down or love for something else.

Paul forced his eyes away from the wheel. He didn't even realize he was running until he heard the sound of his own feet pounding the splintered planks. The ocean thrashed about beside him. Nature, flowing. He ran. Toward lemon Pledge, and the daughter who hated him, and the wife who was not looking at him, Paul ran like a rabbit with a wolf at its heels.

OCTOBER 1995

ELLEN SAID SHE WOULD BRING EVERYTHING THEY needed for their costumes, but she had not told Gary what they were going to be. Gary could not remember the last time he had dressed up for Halloween. College, probably. Typically he kept all the lights off to discourage visitors. This year was going to be different. Weeks ago Ellen had seen the HOA monthly notice clipped to Gary's refrigerator, which included a reminder about trick-or-treating: when it would take place and how to help your children participate safely. She asked if she could spend that evening at his home, in costume, handing out treats to the children of his neighborhood. Trick-or-treating was not big in her neighborhood, she explained, where the homes were spaced out unevenly, lighting was poor, and there were no sidewalks. Gary would, of course, not turn down an evening with Ellen, even if costumes were required.

....

In July and early August they had spent loads of time together. Several nights a week: dinner, sex, TV, ice cream, music, pajamas, breakfast, coffee, newspapers, crosswords, TV, sometimes sex again. Ellen kept saying how much she was enjoying herself. Things had changed though, with the arrival of Ellen's granddaughter. Paul and Corinne were grateful for the help that came with Ellen's presence, so she stayed with them often. She returned to town when school was back in session, and Gary expected they would resume frequent get-togethers, but things had been busy for Ellen since then, working full-time during the week, and she continued to spend most weekends at Paul and Corinne's. Gary missed her. And he had not received an invitation to join her on any of her trips to be with her family. Not that he was itching to go; he wasn't big on babies and thought it might be awkward with Paul and Corinne, but it didn't feel great. Ellen had taken the abacus and reported that Paul and Corinne thought it was beautiful, but Gary didn't know how she would have described the person who made it. A friend? A man?

The afternoon of Halloween, Gary tended his flowers out front. He had a dozen pots of yellow, cream, and burgundy mums. The colors were flamboyant that day, the air cold and invigorating, the sunshine vivid. October was magnificent—it was the one month of the year where nature seemed to hold tangible influence over Gary. He would have enjoyed spending more of it outdoors with Ellen. Early in the month he had suggested a cidery or the flower festival in Ashtabula, but with her busy schedule it just hadn't worked out.

However, he felt that this evening, these final hours of October, held great promise.

....

Ellen arrived at five o'clock with a duffel bag. She was wearing a green sweat suit.

Gary said, "Are you the Hulk?"

She laughed. "You'll see."

In the kitchen she pulled out many different types of bagged candy and emptied them all into a large mixing bowl. She stirred it around with her hand.

Then she pulled out materials for costumes: a bag of balloons, a ziplock filled with safety pins, an oblong basket, several sheets of green felt, and a basketball-sized red sphere that she handled with care.

"Fruit of the Loom," she announced.

Gary said, "Huh."

"I'll be the cluster of grapes. I'll need your help filling these purple balloons and pinning them on. And you"—she held up the red helmet, which he could now see had a brown stem, eye holes, and a large opening at the bottom—"will be the apple."

"I see."

"I'll need you to change into brown clothes," she said. "I know you own plenty of brown. And I'll cut this felt into leaves and pin them on you. When the kids come you'll hold this basket over your shoulder, see? Just like the cornucopia from the logo. I know the basket's not the right shape, but."

Gary picked up the apple helmet. "Good Lord, this thing is heavy."

"I made it out of papier-mâché and had to go really thick so it would hold together and keep its shape even with the holes."

"Good Lord," Gary said again.

Preparing the outfits to Ellen's satisfaction took longer than he would have guessed. By the time they were ready, the sun was low and shadows were long.

Gary had made chicken salad earlier, and they put sandwiches together quickly. Ellen ate standing because she had insisted on full-body coverage with the purple balloons.

A rushed sandwich on foot and in costume was not what Gary had in mind for dinner, but Ellen was so happy, he was determined to be a sport. Besides, the HOA notice said that trick-or-treating would end at seven thirty, so there would be a few hours of potential alone time before Ellen would need to head home to let Rocky out and get herself into bed, since it was a school night. Gary hoped this apple helmet might earn him some time in the bedroom.

Ellen turned on Gary's porch light and she set up a chair for Gary right inside the door because his back was bad and she didn't want him standing the whole time, but she did want them to be in position to answer the door quickly.

Princess Leia and a mouse were the first to arrive, and they seemed mildly frightened by Gary's and Ellen's costumes, more so after Ellen proclaimed, "Fruit of the Loom!"

There was a steady stream of trick-or-treaters for the next hour. The response to their costumes was lackluster, but the enthusiasm for their abundant candy supply and Ellen's permission for them to take several heaping handfuls apiece felt like a success.

Dusk advanced to dark, and eventually after a long spell of no trick-or-treaters, they decided to call it quits.

Gary pulled off the apple helmet, set it on the ground, and smoothed his hair.

He said, "Want some cider?"

In the kitchen Ellen pointed to a new photograph on Gary's refrigerator. "Is that your daughter?"

"It is. And her girlfriend."

"They are so pretty," Ellen said. "Both of them. They make a pretty pair. You must be excited to see them for Christmas."

Gary nodded. He was. And nervous. He had made genuine efforts and real headway in his relationship with his daughter in recent months, which involved apologies for some of his past behavior and frequent phone calls just to chat. Still, he didn't know what it would be like to pal around with these girls. He wondered if they would wear matching pajamas. Also, Gary wasn't thrilled about the agreed-upon schedule; he wasn't going to see them until the twenty-sixth because they would be with his ex and the excavator on Christmas Day. Gary had an open invitation to the Christmas dinner his cousin Susan always hosted for extended family—the event that had resulted in his first date with Ellen— and thought maybe he'd go to that to keep from getting lonely, though it presented its own form of torture.

He said, "Are you hosting Christmas Day like you've been hoping?"

"Yes," Ellen reported happily. "It's finally confirmed. Paul and Corinne and the baby will be with Corinne's family on Christmas Eve, then me all of Christmas Day. And my ex is going to come, too. Just so we don't have to split up the day. We haven't seen each other in ages, but I'm sure it will go fine."

Gary tried to read her exact feelings about this and could not. Or maybe he detected something that he did not wish to acknowledge.

He said, "Good for you. Both of you. I couldn't abide a holiday with my ex even though things are civil. I'd rather take the twenty-sixth, thank for very much." He poured cider into mugs and put them in the microwave. "I guess it's not uncommon though. One of the men at support group the other night said he'll be with his ex for Christmas. He's got a new grandbaby too. Similar situation to yours." An alarming realization snagged hard inside of Gary. "What's your ex's name again?"

"Michael."

"Oh my God," Gary said. A collision of thoughts stormed. "He introduced himself as Mike. Oh God. Gray goatee. Mole under his eye?"

Ellen's face went pale.

"Michael and Mike are very different names," Gary defended himself feebly. "Small town. I don't know how it didn't ever occur ... He never said your name though ..." The microwave beeped and Gary turned away from Ellen to take out the steaming ciders.

"He's shared with your group about me, I take it," she murmured.

"Ellen, I can't talk about that. It's like AA. Unspoken, the confidentiality, but."

Ellen was shaking her head, suddenly vehement. "No. You were saying, he said, about ... You must. I need to know everything he said."

Gary turned away. His eyes focused on the dead leaves pasted to the exterior of the window, one of them splitting at its center vein. "It's an issue of integrity."

Ellen grabbed him by the forearm so that he had to face her. "Gary, you and me are intimate. You don't owe *him* anything!"

He interrupted gently, "I think you know how fond of you I am. Not just fond. I think we are very close."

"Then tell me what Michael said." Her grip was painful now, her posture rigid. "Is it another woman? You know I am still in the dark." She started to cry.

Gary used his free hand to gently pry her fingers from his arm, and he gathered her hands in his. "I can't. I'm sorry. It's not about you. It's not even about Mike. Michael. It's the principle."

Ellen withdrew her hands from his in utter disbelief. Her eyes were watery blades. "I can't believe you're on his team now."

"I'm certainly not," Gary said. "Don't be silly. I won't go back to the group. I will never see him again. I'm with you. I want to be with you."

When she didn't respond to this declaration, Gary moved back to regard her. "But you don't want to be with me, do you? If you had it your way, you'd rather get back together with Michael."

Ellen took a step away from him. "Not necessarily," she said.

"You want me to tell you what the problem was, according to Michael, so that you can fix it."

She said, "Not necessarily," again, after a pause.

Gary said, "You don't want me to meet your granddaughter." Until these words left his mouth, Gary hadn't realized how much he cared.

"What? That just hasn't worked out, the timing," Ellen said.

"Because you don't want it to work out."

"This isn't about her," Ellen looked genuinely bewildered by the direction the argument had taken. She looked at him. "Are you really upset about not meeting her? You don't even like babies! It's certainly not personal."

That was horseshit, Gary thought. Every moment in life: personal. What else could it ever be? But if Ellen was hell-bent on maintaining her most aggrieved status here, so be it. He said, "If you are so obsessed with finding out what Michael is saying and thinking and doing with his life, why don't you call the psychic hotline about it instead of hounding me?"

She looked at him stupidly like, *You think I haven't thought of that?*

Gary knew their relationship had cracked. He said, "My actual point is if you're still this obsessed with Michael, you probably shouldn't be here, or with me, at all."

"You've turned this all around."

"Nah," Gary said, coldly. "I've got it right."

"Fine. If you want me to leave I will."

When she began to gather her things, Gary did not speak nor did he make a move to stop her, but he unpinned one of the green felt leaves from his brown shirt and handed it to her. She said, "Oh for heaven's sake," like it was a ridiculous gesture, but then she did wait for him to unpin and return the rest.

She packed these and the apple helmet and everything else into her duffel.

He watched out the window as she tottered down the path, then tangled awkwardly with purple balloons in order to get into her car.

Her headlights flicked on and then she was gone.

Gary turned out all the lights in his house, went to the dark living room, and sat alone with his thoughts.

He thought of the bottle of port wine that was in the basement. It was the only alcohol in the house. He had kept it because it was expensive, a gift he had received for his retirement years ago.

Retirement had been tough on Gary, which was strange since he had spent his entire career complaining about his job. But retirement was when he found himself making daily excuses to start drinking earlier and earlier, until it was rare that he wasn't tanked by noon. When his relationships started to suffer—most notably, of course, his marriage—things went from bad to worse. He had come to hate himself thoroughly. Then his wife left him. Why on earth would she stay? His heart became a tangled black ball, a snarl of bad arteries. One day, he seriously considered taking his life. He thought that there was nothing worth seeing or doing or feeling anymore. But something or someone, from his past or his future, summoned him out of that place in that moment and he hadn't returned.

He'd come a long way since then. But damn if he wasn't feeling sorry for himself right now.

Gary's mind traveled from his own journey to the support group sessions that Michael had attended and the things Michael had said.

The boring and terrible truth was that Michael had left Ellen for the same reason people nearly always left each other: because he thought he could do better. In certain departments. Or in Michael's case—in his view—one department in particular. This information was unoriginal and uninteresting but would have nevertheless crushed Ellen.

When Michael had shared his story and these words, they had not incited any strong reaction from Gary. He felt a certain kinship with all of the men who attended the sessions, simply by virtue of their shared vulnerability; he did not judge the stories told at support group, even when it seemed clear that the man had been in the wrong—which was more often than not the case. Now, though, thinking of these words, *I can do better*, applied to Ellen, Gary thought they were the cruelest words ever to exist and Michael the cruelest man.

Michael had expressed to the group that he was not exactly remorseful for having left his wife, but he also wasn't any happier than he'd been while married—and that was why he sought out the support group. After a number of failed attempts at dating women who met the criteria that he believed his wife was lacking, he was waffling on the course forward and found himself missing her companionship. He reported to the group that he had been gentle enough with the divorce conversation and proceedings that he thought the door was not completely shut to a reconciliation with his ex. Gary thought it was obvious the guy was depressed, and like Gary's, his misery had little to do with his wife, or the department in which she was supposedly lacking, or his failed dating relationships since splitting with her. It didn't seem clear to Michael though. And as far as Gary could recall, it wasn't clear whether Michael's realization that he probably could not do better than his wife was a product of new appreciation for her or a recognition of his own depreciating value in the dating market. Either way, Michael had told the group that he was fairly confident his ex would be receptive to reconciliation, especially if they had a nice Christmas—it would be the first family get-together since the divorce. There would be a new baby there, he explained, which would have everyone in extra-good spirits. At the time, Gary had thought toward Michael, *Good for you.* Now, Gary thought: *Fuck you! Fuck you! Fuck you!*

But Gary wouldn't tell Ellen any of this. He would not provide her with this information as either a means of reassurance or as a warning; he would not advise or console her. He would not attempt to convince her that she could do better than Michael. She needed to live her life and make her decisions with the knowledge and memories she already had.

A few minutes later there was a knock at Gary's door. He got up quickly to answer, with the happy idea that it could be Ellen. He hoped she might have gotten halfway home, gotten to thinking straight, and reached some cooperative understanding about Gary's refusal to disclose what Michael said in the sessions. More importantly, he hoped she might have realized she was missing Gary the way he was missing her. She might have even realized that she could do better than Michael.

But that knock was more forceful than he would expect from Ellen. And Gary had not seen the flash of headlights. So at the front door, Gary peered through the peephole instead of opening blindly.

He had to adjust his gaze downward to identify the knocker.

There were three of them: a Hamburglar, a robot, and a Scooby-Doo. They were small enough that Gary was surprised there was no parent accompanying them. They were standing expectantly with little plastic pumpkin buckets full of candy.

Gary did not open the door but kept watching them through the peephole.

After a bit, Scooby-Doo scratched his blue collar and said, "Let's keep going."

The robot said, "My mom says the guy who lives here is an asshole, anyway."

Gary watched as the Hamburglar squatted over the pot of

yellow mums nearest the door for a few seconds, snickering, then they all scampered off. Gary didn't think the kid was there long enough to actually shit, but he wouldn't know for sure until he checked tomorrow.

ROB HAD BEEN DATING THIS KAI WOMAN FOR ONLY A little over a month and already she was making crazy demands. Apparently she did not have a family of her own to celebrate Thanksgiving with. And when Rob extended Janet's generous invite for Kai to join their family for the traditional meal Janet always prepared, Kai said that she would be glad to make the trip with Rob (whose sons would be with their mother on Thanksgiving Day) but suggested that, instead of a traditional feast, the whole family volunteer to help serve the Thanksgiving meal offered at the soup kitchen. Apparently Kai was vegan, so she wouldn't eat much of a traditional meal anyway. And she had already done the research to know where the soup kitchen was located in their town and what a volunteer shift on Thanksgiving would look like.

If only Janet had Paul and Corinne to use as her excuse to do the normal thing, but this year they would take the baby and be with Paul's mother, Ellen. So Janet told herself she must make the best of this. It was good Rob was dating again, especially now that his ex was engaged. And Janet liked the idea of another family wedding.

Furthermore, she didn't want to scare Rob off of a visit home, because she really needed to sit him down to talk about Bruce's memory loss. She and Bruce had decided to hold off until Olivia was born and then decided not to do it during Rob's birthday weekend at the Shore because they didn't want it to overshadow the celebration. They hadn't seen Rob in person since, and it was clearly a conversation that should take place face-to-face. Rob and Kai planned to stay for the whole weekend, and Rob had said that the Friday after Thanksgiving Kai would be taking the car for the day to do something by herself. Janet figured that would be the perfect time to call Corinne over to the house and tell both of the kids that their father was losing it.

Rob and Kai arrived after dinnertime the night before Thanksgiving.

Janet watched out the window, and her first thought was that they must have invited Kai's mother, too.

The woman who got out of the passenger door had extremely long white hair that swirled majestically around her head. She was at least six feet tall, Janet guessed, and thin as a whisker. She wore what appeared to be a lightweight blue cape made of billowy material. She and Rob kissed and held hands as they made their way up the walk to the house. Bruce was across the room and Janet hissed in a loud whisper, "They're here and she is *old*, oh my word, don't you dare say anything rude about it."

Rob did introductions. He seemed nervous.

On the phone he had said to Janet that things were moving really quickly. He had also mentioned that Kai was a model. Janet had therefore harbored two major concerns: that Kai would be inappropriately young for Rob or that he had already gotten her pregnant. Janet permitted herself a little giggle about this now.

Rob said they were pretty beat after a long day in the car and they weren't hungry, so they'd probably turn in early since tomorrow would be a full day.

Janet eyed him. "All righty then."

Kai said, "Your home is so lovely."

"Get yourselves settled," Janet said. "I'll put out a snack."

Janet couldn't help making big eyes at Bruce when Rob's and Kai's backs were turned. Bruce seemed totally unfazed, and Janet thought he probably didn't get it.

Janet watched as they made their way down the hall to Rob's childhood bedroom, where he always stayed. She wondered what Kai would think of Rob's lava lamp, which Janet had put on a few hours ago so it would be warm and active by the time they arrived.

Janet went to the kitchen and returned with a dish of nuts and some gummy candies. The nuts she knew were vegan. The gummies, she wasn't sure. She thought she'd heard such things contained horse bones. She had a colorful combination of worms and whales. On the coffee table, though, the gummies looked plain ridiculous, so she bagged them back up even though they were Rob's favorites. She'd offer them another time.

Rob and Kai returned to the living room. Kai had secured her long white hair up in a knot high on her head with a clip. Janet was impressed with the way Kai made their yucky old sectional look like an expensive piece of furniture simply by sitting on it. She certainly had the looks and the grace and the effortless affect of a model. But, Janet wondered, for whom? Metamucil?

Kai took a handful of nuts.

Janet clapped her hands together. "So! How did you two meet?"

Rob turned to Kai. "You want to? Or you want me to?"

Kai was chewing slowly and gestured for him to go on ahead.

Rob said, "At the grocery store. She was loading her car and the bag busted and everything went everywhere. I picked up a can of beans that rolled into my foot. Love at first sight."

"The lady or the beans?" Bruce said. Janet looked at him. It was very rare of Bruce to pipe up this way. It was actually a pretty good joke. But was it a joke?

Everyone laughed.

Janet said, "That is a cute story, though."

"I know it is," Rob said.

Janet turned to Kai. "Tell me everything about yourself, from the very beginning."

"I'm from Oregon originally," Kai said. "My parents split early on."

Janet said, "Wow, okay, taking me back all the way."

Kai continued, "So it was just my mother and me and my brother. We moved around a fair amount. She did the best she could."

Kai spoke about her love of art in school and the jewelry making she did to support herself for a number of years after graduating.

Janet said, "Did you make that?"

Kai was wearing a large and ornate pendant around her neck. She touched it like she had to remember, then said yes.

"Very nice," Janet said. "It is actually remarkable what it does with the light."

Bruce said, "Very nice," with his eyebrows arched high.

To Janet's shock, she realized he might be trying to flirt with Kai.

Rob said, "You should see her whole collection, it's really something."

Janet said, "And that's what you do for work now, then? For a living? Oh, and Rob said you model."

"Not much of that anymore," Kai said. "Mostly just the jewelry."

"You must fetch a lot for them."

"Well," Kai dusted salt from her fingers. "Also, I was married for a number of years. Our settlement was substantial."

"Ah," Janet said. "As was his"—she nodded in Rob's direction—"as I'm sure he has told you." Janet helped herself to some nuts.

They chatted for a while longer. Rob filled his parents in on how the twins were doing.

Janet said grimly, "When do we get those boys for Thanksgiving?"

"Next year," Rob said. "Get used to it, Mom. How are Paul and Corinne doing?" He turned to Kai to remind her, "My sister. She's got the baby. You'll meet them later this weekend."

Janet said, "They're fine. I'd like to see more of them. Ellen—you know, Paul's mother—lives two hours away and gets more time with them than I do, I swear. Well, anyway, you know how it is with a baby. Somebody is always fussing. And half the time it's not the baby."

Eventually Rob and Kai went to bed. Janet said to Bruce, "Somebody had an extra little spring in their step tonight." He didn't respond, and she didn't pester him further. She was in high spirits herself, thinking maybe Kai would offer her a pendant for hosting this weekend.

. . . .

In the morning, Janet reported to Rob and Kai as coffee brewed that Bruce had slept on his hip wrong and it was hurting him this morning and he wasn't going to come to the soup kitchen after all. He would need to spend the day on his back instead of his feet.

Rob said, "I hate for Dad to be alone on Thanksgiving. Maybe we should all hang back, spend the day here."

Janet lifted a shoulder, indicating her receptiveness to a change of plans. She looked back and forth between Rob and Kai. She had a few frozen pizzas and things for a vegan salad on hand just in case something like this happened, but decided not to say so until Kai weighed in.

Kai said, "I'd feel too bad backing out after getting us all set up with Wanda at the kitchen." She poured herself some coffee. "If you two want to stay here, I understand."

Rob said, "No, no. We should go. You're so right, babe."

The immediacy with which Rob fell in line with Kai instantly erased the goodwill Janet had developed for her overnight.

Janet stood around in her pajamas a little bit longer to see if there was a change of heart, but there was not, even after she mentioned once again how much pain Bruce was in.

The soup kitchen operated out of the basement of the large Methodist church. It was a zoo of volunteers sipping coffee, staring at clipboards, putting on HELLO sticker name tags, getting assigned to stations, washing hands, donning hairnets.

The basement smelled of dirty diapers. They were playing Christmas music over the intercom, jazzy piano renditions of classic hymns. Rob, Kai, and Janet were assigned to corn. Rob opened the gallon-sized cans with the industrial opener, Kai strained, and Janet scooped and dumped into the serving vats. It was too noisy for them to chat with one another. Janet looked around from time to time and was astonished by the volume of food they were preparing. She wouldn't have guessed there were more than about three homeless people in town.

Just before noon, Wanda announced with a megaphone that there was a line around the block and it was time to check in with supervisors for serving station assignments. Rob ended up near the entrance, handing out sanitary hand wipes. Kai was assigned to the farthest end, with whipped cream. Janet was in the middle, on gravy. There were far more volunteers than they would have needed. She could have single-handedly done both potatoes and gravy. Instead there were six do-gooders crammed in there with their ladles and spoons and jolly attitudes. The stupidity of it all made Janet want to spit.

But Janet's opinion of the whole operation changed once she was actually serving food to needy people. They were so polite it broke her heart.

For a little while, she harbored the notion of volunteering here on a regular basis. Feeling softer toward Kai for initiating this activity, Janet glanced down in her direction and was taken aback by what she observed. The man Kai was serving leaned forward to whisper something in Kai's ear, and in response, Kai pretended to lick the spoon of whipped cream that she held, in what could only be described as a sexual manner. The man laughed bawdily, exposing dark gums.

The next person in line was a younger man with his hair in a mohawk, who lingered after getting his whipped cream to chat with Kai. Kai must be telling him the greatest jokes ever told, Janet thought, from the way he laughed. He stayed and stayed.

Janet watched in a trance that was broken only when a guest standing before her said, "Gravy, please, ma'am. Gravy?"

Eventually the pace of service slowed as they neared the end of the line. Wanda made her way through volunteers, releasing them in shifts to get their own meal and encouraging them to sit among the guests, to mingle.

Janet was going to see if Rob and Kai wanted to join her and sit together at an empty table she had scoped out, but when she looked down to the dessert station, she saw that Kai had already been released from her duties and was no longer there. Janet searched the line for her, then the room, and eventually spotted her at a faraway table, sitting next to mohawk man. Of course, there was no plate before Kai—she probably wouldn't touch any of this food with a ten-foot pole—but she was sipping from a Styrofoam cup and listening intently to whatever the man was saying. Her lanky frame was draped toward him in an intimate manner, and her loose-fitting shirt was falling off one shoulder, exposing a black bra strap. She had taken off her hairnet and released her white hair in all its splendor. Janet couldn't peel her eyes away. She looked for Rob. He was talking with Wanda right now, handing over his box of leftover wipes.

Janet decided to go intercept Rob right away, to initiate getting a plate together, and she would use this as an excuse to point out Kai. She did not want Rob to miss this.

Unfortunately, though, when Janet looked back, Kai was already vacating that table. Janet watched a moment longer and was stunned to see not just a farewell but a kiss between Kai and mohawk man. On the lips.

Janet felt like her own head was about to pop off her neck. She looked at Rob. She looked at Kai. Then she ran to Rob.

He said, "Hey, Mom. Are you—"

Janet announced, "Your girlfriend just kissed a homeless man on the mouth."

Rob threw his head back to laugh.

Janet blinked. "That's funny?"

"You're ridiculous," he said.

"It's true! That man with the mohawk. Go ask!"

"Mom, I know you're bitter about spending the day here."

"I'm thrilled to be here! Are you kidding? I love volunteering. That's got nothing to do with it. It happened! Ask him. Ask *her*. Here she comes."

Kai had spotted them, waved, and strode over.

Rob said, "I will."

"Good!" Janet was ready to explode with righteous fury.

When Kai approached, Rob said, "My mom thinks she just caught you making out with some guy."

Janet scoffed, "I didn't say *making out*, Robert." She looked at Kai but suddenly felt too shy to meet her eyes. "I said you shared a kiss."

Kai spoke calmly, "I suppose that's true. He told me his story. How he ended up without a home and no place to eat on Thanksgiving."

"Why," Janet demanded, "did he tell *you* the story?"

"I'm not sure," Kai said. "Because I acted like I was interested, I imagine. Actually I shouldn't say that. I *was* interested. It was an interesting story."

Janet suddenly felt hopeless. "The kiss?" she muttered.

"I told him I was going to come find my boyfriend to eat with, and

I wished him well," Kai said. "He just sort of leaned in. Or up. I didn't ask for it or enjoy it, being kissed, if that's what you're implying."

Janet said, "Well, from where I was standing, I couldn't tell."

"A little mouth peck is normal in some cultures," Kai pointed out evenly.

"Is that some *modeling* thing?" Janet struck her own pose.

"Not at all. I just didn't want . . . Hm. I guess I didn't want him to think I thought I was better than him. So I just let it happen."

Kai looked at Rob, who looked at his mother.

Rob said, "Are you happy, Janet?"

"You know I hate when you call me that," Janet snapped. "You two go on ahead and eat and have your nice time. *Mingle*, if that's what the kids are calling it these days. I'm ready to leave anytime. I'm going to step outside. I'm having a hot flash."

Janet threw her hairnet in the trash on her way out.

She stood by herself in an empty stairwell. It was very cold outside, but she was, in fact, having a hot flash, so the air felt good on her cheeks. She thought unhappily of Paul and Corinne and Olivia eating turkey and stuffing and pie with Ellen.

She could hear muffled Christmas music from inside; this had to be the eighth time through the same album. Janet didn't have any great love for Christmas music, or music in general. A number of times over the course of their marriage, Bruce had been brought to tears by music. At least she thought that was the case, because music was always the common denominator, whether it was a hymn at church or a ballad on the radio or one of the kids' school concerts, some brassy, cacophonous rendition of "John Jacob Jingleheimer." It always caught Janet by surprise to discover her husband wiping his eyes. She couldn't relate to him in these moments; she felt extremely far away—left behind, really—when he went to this place of beauty where she did not know how to join him. It was crazy to say, but Bruce's tears over music made Janet feel more jealous than any other woman ever had.

Janet was pulled from these thoughts when the door she was leaning against suddenly opened behind her, prompting her to nearly fall back inside on her ass, but instead she fell into Kai's arms.

Kai steadied her, stepped out, and pulled the door shut behind them.

Janet stared coolly out into the parking lot.

"I'm having a hot flash, too," Kai said.

Janet wouldn't look at her.

Kai said, "I'm not upset about what you said. I know you're just looking out for your kid."

Janet said, "Oh, whatever." She took a few deep breaths and got herself calmed down. "You're right though, that's all I was doing." Recognizing that they still had the full weekend ahead of them, Janet was now eager to be at peace and offered up some small talk. "Rob says you're taking the car for the day tomorrow. Where you off to?"

"I thought I'd go to Dry Creek Park."

"I remember now, he did tell me that. He said you wanted to do some hiking by yourself."

"It's something I do every year on the twenty-fifth."

"What's the occasion?"

"My daughter's birthday."

"You have a daughter? Rob didn't tell me."

"Well, I didn't raise her. We don't have a relationship. I had her when I was fourteen and gave her up for adoption."

"*Fourteen*," Janet gasped. "My stars. The father . . ." She didn't finish the question. She didn't want to feel pain.

Kai lifted one shoulder. "Just some kid. A friend of my brother's."

Janet wondered about more things relating to that, but instead she asked, "What's your daughter like?"

"I haven't got a clue. She's turning forty-three today. Apparently she has a child of her own," Kai said. "But I haven't met them in person. My child or her child."

"My stars," Janet said again.

"My daughter doesn't want to meet," Kai said. "I keep hoping that'll change. At this point I don't imagine it will. I reach out with a phone call every few years but don't push it beyond that. I only know I have a grandchild because the child answered the last time I called."

Janet had no idea what to say.

"I get sad every year on her birthday," Kai explained. "Thinking about giving birth all those years ago. How I . . ." Kai's voice trembled then shrank away entirely. She cleared her throat and added, "It goes best if I spend the day by myself."

Janet said, "I shouldn't have pried. When Rob said you were going to be on your own for the day, he didn't tell me any of this, just that you wanted to go for a hike by yourself. Does he know why?"

"Yes. But I don't think he really gets it."

"No," Janet said. "I don't imagine he does."

It had become overcast, and the sky was low and gray. A stray cat trotted by and paused to bare its sharp teeth at them. Janet rubbed her hands together for warmth, and her skin was so dry it sounded like sandpaper. She thought about her own birth, to a mother who did not want her or like her or love her. Janet knew the doctors and scientists and experts would laugh their butts off if she were ever to assert this aloud, but she could swear to God that she remembered the day—or days, rather, because apparently labor had taken that long—that she was born. Janet could remember her entry and introduction to this world because she still felt those same feelings to this day. She felt them all the time, actually. People were constantly saying and doing things that brought it all back, again and again.

The door opened behind them and Rob appeared. "You two make up?" he said. "Do I need to go beat up a man with a mohawk for trying to steal my lady and offending my mother?"

Janet said, "Give it a rest."

Rob laughed. "Mom, I think we'll drop you off at home then go for a drive. I want to show Kai around town."

"Did you already have your meal here?"

"One bite of turkey about made me puke. Texture like gum. Just kept chewing. We'll pick up smoothies or something." Rob was carrying Kai's coat draped over his arm. He said to her, "You having one, too?"

Janet wasn't sure what he was talking about until she noticed that Kai was fanning her flushed face.

Rob patted his pocket, where his keys jingled. "Okay, ladies, let's get moving."

He dropped Janet at home and said he and Kai would be back in time for dinner, but he didn't specify a time.

Janet said, "Very good. We'll have salad. Don't rush."

Bruce was in bed but awake, propped halfway upright with pillows and paging through one of Janet's old *People* magazines.

She said, "Hi, honey, how's your hip?"

"I'm all right. How was your event?"

"You know what, it was really nice," Janet said. "It's good to help the needy. You should do it sometime. You want something to eat?"

Bruce shook his head. "That pain pill you gave me made me so tired. I think I'll probably knock off again soon."

"Holler if you need anything. We've got a few hours before Rob and your girlfriend get back."

"You mean his girlfriend," Bruce said.

Janet patted his feet through the comforter. "If you say so."

She put together a sandwich in the kitchen, then settled herself on the couch. It had started to rain. Then right before her eyes, it turned to snow. She watched this for a while, then turned on the TV. Unfortunately the Macy's Thanksgiving Day Parade was over. There was nothing else she was much interested in watching, but she kept it on anyway. One minute it was a sitcom, the next minute it was a different sitcom, then it was the news, then a woman selling bracelets, and the living room was dark, and Janet was cold. Apparently, many hours had passed. It had all come at her so fast. She had no idea how much of it she had spent awake.

DECEMBER 1995

PART 1

JANET SAID, "I CANNOT GET OVER THE NAME THING. I can't, I won't."

"How's that?"

"Them picking a name that means nothing. Belongs to nobody. Not *nobody*-nobody, but nobody we know. Just because they like it. They think it *sounds* nice. Woo-hoo." She wiggled her fingers in the air. "Also I think if they didn't hold her constantly, she wouldn't demand to be constantly held. Don't get me started on that. But it's the name thing that's really got my goat today. Are you listening? It just would have been nice, is all I'm saying, to have a family name. Oh well. I must get over it." Janet brushed down the hairs on her arm. "I forget, who were you named after, honey?"

"No one that I know," Bruce said.

Janet squinted. "Really?"

"I don't believe so."

"I doubt they chose *Bruce* for the way it sounds."

She went to the bookshelf on the far wall and pulled an encyclopedia from it. She leafed through for a bit, dragged her finger down a page. "Aha," she said. "I found out what *Bruce* means. 'From the brushwood thicket.'" She closed the encyclopedia. "I think that suits you." She returned to the couch. "My name means 'a gift from God.'"

Bruce reached for the notebook that lived on the end table next to his chair. His handwriting was getting worse and worse but he was determined to keep writing.

After making a note, his eyes traveled to the top of the page, where asterisks surrounded the words, in all caps and his own handwriting: *Harry is dead.* Bruce felt confusion, followed by a crest of sorrow and remorse. For what? He looked up from the notebook, for Janet, and found her on the couch. He said, "My brother, Harry?"

"Dead." Janet didn't look up. "Long time ago."

Bruce looked back down at his notebook.

Janet said, "I told you to write it at the top of a bunch of pages in your notebook because you keep forgetting. Bringing him up. Just in the last couple weeks, since the Christmas decorations went up. I was hoping if you saw it in your own writing every day it would sink in. Seems like it's not sinking in."

"I remember now," Bruce said. This was his default response these days.

Oh, Harry, his big brother, a good brother and a good man. Right?

. . . .

Harry had served in World War II while Bruce was too young for the draft. Bruce's guilt over this was made worse by Harry's assignment, which landed him in ground combat.

Harry was a newlywed when he left, and when he returned he was such a different man that his wife left him. He did not remarry. He moved around for some years then settled in South Bend, Indiana, where he worked for an auto parts manufacturer. It was a five-hour drive from Bruce and Janet, so the brothers did not see a whole lot of each other but spoke on the phone now and then. From their phone conversations Bruce did not perceive enough of a difference in his brother since the war that he could understand why Harry's wife left, though he knew it was a different matter entirely to live with someone.

For a number of years Bruce extended invites to Harry for the holidays, not knowing what sort of a time Harry was having by himself in South Bend. Harry always declined, explaining that he didn't get paid time off, so it was hard to justify the trip. Finally, though, one year when Christmas fell on a weekend, Harry announced that he would join Bruce's family. He would get in on Christmas Eve and stay for several days.

Harry arrived late in the afternoon, delayed by some snow on his route.

He had brought presents for the kids—Rob was fifteen, Corinne was seven—which he put under the tree with all the others.

Janet was visibly delighted by Harry's enjoyment of the meal she served that evening.

Harry had always been a wonderful storyteller, and he regaled the family with hilarious tales. Bruce laughed and laughed at his brother's stories, and while he laughed he looked around the table at the others all laughing. He felt so festive that he had a little bit more to drink than he usually would. With Janet's approval, Bruce poured a small amount of beer for Rob, who had only ever taken sips before.

Bruce got to thinking how great it would be if his brother would move to town. He wondered if anything was keeping Harry in South Bend other than the job. He thought if Harry lived here, they could watch baseball games together on TV and grill burgers on sunny weekends. Bruce thought how amazing it would be to have a friend.

While Janet cleaned up the meal and Corinne sat at the piano to play the few carols she had learned, Harry initiated a game of poker with Bruce and Rob.

Rob had never played before and Bruce had only played a few times, back in his twenties and never for money, so Harry took them through the rules. He wrote up little cards detailing the hierarchy of hands. He said he had learned to play when he was in the military to pass time and blow off steam but had barely touched cards since.

Rob asked his uncle how long he'd served.

Believing Harry's service might be a sore subject—or could lead to one—Bruce interrupted to offer more beer.

Rob asked again and Harry said, "Year and a half."

"Did you kill anybody?"

Bruce said, "Robbie, let's keep it light."

Harry turned to his nephew and shrugged. "Guess those stories will have to wait."

"I can handle it," Rob urged. His young face was flushed with excitement. Never once had Rob asked Bruce to elaborate on a story from his life.

Harry said, "I'm sure you could. But doesn't look like your father's got the stomach for it, least not tonight."

Bruce squeaked air in through his teeth. "Another time."

"Okay, okay, okay," Harry said. "Let's play some cards."

Bruce figured they would just have fun with it, no real money, but Harry insisted they'd have more fun if actual stakes were involved, even if they were low.

They decided to start with coins. Bruce and Janet had a large jar, and Harry would trade in with cash.

By the time they got around to actually starting a game, it was time for Janet to take Corinne to bed. Over her shoulder, Janet called, "I'm gonna turn in soon, too. Don't you boys stay up late, and don't touch anything in the fridge that's for tomorrow. None of that meat."

They did a few trial hands, then started the actual betting.

For a while, it was good fun as fortune favored them all equally; the same small pile of coins got passed around and around and around.

Beer, too, got passed around and around.

When Harry got up for another drink, he peered into the refrigerator and said, "What would happen if I ate the whole Christmas dinner tonight and blamed it on Santa?"

Bruce said, "If you want to see a woman turn into a devil in front of your eyes, go ahead."

Rob snorted into his fist.

Bruce never joked about Janet like this. It pleased him to get a laugh out of his son.

Harry got a little more aggressive with his next few bets and had a few wins. Then quite a few more. Soon the entire coin jar was in play and then that was not enough.

Bruce could see Rob getting frustrated. He was exhaling noisily and clawing at his pimples.

Bruce said maybe they ought to call it a night, but Harry said he had plenty of cash from his Christmas bonus; he offered to divide that up and put it in play, keeping tabs on who owed him what.

Bruce left it up to Rob whether they would continue, thinking his son would be ready to bow out after the losses. But to Bruce's surprise Rob was keen to keep playing.

Rob said, "Can't expect me to quit while I'm behind."

Bruce said, "I was happy to spot you coins, but if we're talking more money than that, you're on your own, buddy-boy."

During the summer Rob mowed lawns for money and squirreled most of it away for savings. Bruce thought if Rob was determined to keep playing, let him see how quickly all those miserable hours in the hot sun—all of that honest work—could evaporate on the gambling table.

Rob went to his room to retrieve his own cash, and Bruce got out a bag of pretzels.

When Rob returned, Harry counted and distributed piles of cash.

Bruce was surprised how much Rob brought to the table. He said, "That's gotta be about all your savings."

Rob said, "Earned it myself, didn't I?"

Harry said, "Attaboy!" and slapped his nephew on the back.

Bruce wished they were all asleep.

When they started up again, Harry resumed his aggressive play but got a few bad hands in a row and Rob got a couple lucky ones, which he played just right. In no time at all, Rob had cleaned out his father and his uncle of the cash.

Rob's eyes were wide as he looked over his spoils. "It might be almost enough for a new bike," he said. Bruce and Janet had broken the news a while back that Rob would not be getting one for Christmas—it was not in their budget.

Harry took it all well. He was laughing and complimenting his nephew's play.

Bruce felt relieved at the prospect that this would draw the game to a close even if it was not the desired outcome.

But once again when he suggested they call it quits, Harry and Rob overruled him. Bruce opened another beer in order to feel more fun and less anxious.

Harry passed out more cash, tallied, and wrote down new numbers of who owed what.

Play became competitive once again. A few hands went to Bruce, then a few to Harry.

On and on they went, with win streaks and turns in the tide. After another beer, things began to feel lighter and easier to Bruce.

Out of nowhere Rob made a huge bet, pushing everything he had to the center of the table. Bruce knew he was trying to secure the bike; this would be more than enough.

Bruce immediately folded. He turned to Harry and watched as Harry examined his nephew's face, then called his bluff.

Bruce saw his son falter. There was a dramatic moment.

Rob slumped and his hands went to his face as Harry took it all—every penny on the table. Harry scooped up the cash in one swoop and silently arranged it by denominations.

"Well," Bruce said, "that's the way she goes."

Rob's hairline was damp with sweat and his eyelids drooped. Bruce realized that on top of this devastating episode, his son might be quite drunk. He felt stupid and naive for allowing any of this to happen.

Bruce looked at Harry, who appeared uncomfortable with his win but also was not making moves or an offer to just call it a wash and return everyone's money. Bruce was oddly a little hurt by the idea that Harry was really going to keep it all, but then he thought Harry was right; this was the honorable and correct thing to do, between men.

"Well," Bruce broke the tense air around the table, "look at that, almost midnight. Better get to bed before we scare off Santa."

Rob lumbered off toward his room without a word.

Bruce called, "Robbie?" behind him but Rob did not turn back.

Harry and Bruce looked at each other. Harry said, "Got a little carried away, I guess."

Bruce wasn't quite sure what to feel. He said, "I'll get the sheets."

Earlier in the evening they had offered Harry to stay in Rob's room, with Rob on the couch, but Harry had insisted they not go to that trouble.

When Bruce returned to the living room, Harry had already changed into pajamas and set up the pullout.

They spread the sheets together. Bruce said, "More blankets in that cabinet, if you need."

Harry cupped his ear. "You're mumbling."

Bruce pointed and raised his voice. "More blankets in there."

"Hey." Harry cocked his head. "We good?"

"Sure."

"Is it . . . Oh, Bruce. Is it the money?"

"What? No, no," Bruce said. "Fair's fair."

"It is," Harry insisted, "isn't it?" He stared at his brother and smacked his own forehead. "I wasn't *actually* going to keep your kid's money. I was gonna return it all right there, right after it

happened, but the look on your face made me think twice, like you
wanted him to sit with the loss."

"Oh, I see," Bruce said. He felt consoled by this information.
"I guess I do."

Harry said again, "I was never actually going to keep it." He
made a crazy face. "Jesus, Bruce. I'll find some fun way to give it
back tomorrow, stuff it in his stocking or something. I don't actually want Rob's mowing money. Make me feel like a monster. You
thought I was actually gonna do for keeps?"

Bruce laughed. "Okay, okay."

Harry said "Jesus!" again, and they both laughed more before
bidding each other goodnight.

Janet stirred when Bruce crawled into bed.

She said, "You smell like beer."

"I had a few."

She leaned closer. Bruce was expecting more in the way of a
reprimand, or a comment about his breath, but what he received
instead was a kiss.

Then she huffed over onto her side and fell back to sleep.

Bruce reveled in gratitude and his love for her and everyone
else in the home. He thought how nice it would be to watch Harry
return Rob's money tomorrow, better yet if those two formed a
bond over this and other things this weekend. The more good men
Rob had in his life to look up to the better.

Bruce had to shift around awhile to accommodate his back,
which was sore on account of some extra work at the church this
past week. They'd had the kids do all sorts of Christmas crafts in
Sunday school, which resulted in messes of shredded paper and
hardened glue and paint stains. Then there was the trail of melted

wax down the center aisle in the sanctuary, from Advent candles carried at an angle. Then there were all the extra treats around—sprinkle cookies and gingerbread and candied nuts—that left sugar on tables and carpets and pews. It was a lot for Bruce to manage on his own. He didn't get overtime pay but usually they gave him some kind of recognition around Christmas, like a loaf of bread or an ornament. He hadn't received anything yet this year but was sure it was coming.

Eventually Bruce eased into a position that was comfortable enough, and when he fell into sleep he fell hard.

So when he wakened sometime later to a clatter and a thud, he had no clue what planet he was on, much less what had produced the noise.

He rubbed his eyes. The digital clock read 3:16. Janet was sound asleep. The noise could have been a dream, he thought, and rolled over to get back to sleep.

But then he heard more noise—some sort of scuffle.

As best as Bruce could tell, the noise came from the living room, where Harry was sleeping on the pullout couch. So Bruce's first bleary idea was that Harry might have tripped over something like the cord for the plug-in lights on the tree.

Then there were muffled voices. Or just one voice.

Or was it the TV? Harry had had trouble sleeping and turned on a program?

It went quiet, then the voice returned, and although it was not loud, some inexplicable menace accompanied it. Or Bruce was experiencing some inexplicable dread. Or both. Was he still drunk?

Bruce got out of bed, closing the door quietly behind him so that Janet would not waken.

From midway down the hall he could tell that the TV was not on and neither were any of the lights. The voices, if they were ever there, had gone quiet.

Bruce reached the entry to the living room and peered in.

Something moved. Bruce was suddenly thrumming with adrenaline.

It was very dark, but Bruce could see two bodies on the floor next to the pullout couch, in some intimate pose. He could not identify or understand anything beyond the intimacy.

His insides were galloping.

He squinted and eventually was able to make more sense of the scene before him. Harry was kneeling behind Rob, who was seated. Both were facing Bruce. Harry's left elbow was bent around Rob's throat in a tight headlock. Rob's pale face looked bloated and was frozen in terror.

Harry registered Bruce's presence in the hall and he growled, "Kid was going through my stuff."

Bruce felt his own hands extend out from his body in some sort of a gesture. What was this gesture meant to convey? Caution? Kindliness? A veiled threat?

Bruce took a step forward. His eyes were adjusting to the darkness and now he could see Harry's face clearly. Harry's lips were pulled back from his teeth in a gruesome sneer.

Rob appeared to be struggling for air, his mouth open and toothless and black.

Bruce was leaping, lurching, wailing, writhing within his own skin. He took another step forward. He said, "Harry, let my son go."

"Your son?" Harry said, with some measure of disbelief. He looked back down at Rob and repeated his claim, "Kid was sneaking around, going through my stuff."

"Dad," Rob choked, "I wasn't. I was just going to the kitchen for something to eat."

"Liar," Harry growled, and Bruce saw his brother's grip tighten around Rob's neck.

Rob winced and coughed. One of his legs twitched.

Bruce gasped, "For God's sake, Harry! He can't breathe!"

Emotionless, Harry stated, "He knows where I keep the cash."

Bruce watched as Rob meekly attempted to shake his head back and forth, as though to repudiate Harry's account of things. Bruce pleaded silently with Rob to stop this nonsense. He could not look at his son's face.

Bruce begged his own body to produce a calm and firm voice when he said, "Harry, let him go. However it got to this, we'll talk about it. We'll make things right. Just let my kid go."

Harry's eyes were ferocious. "This is no kid! And you—" Harry's expression morphed unnaturally, then abruptly drained of its anger. He gazed down at Rob, then up at Bruce, with genuine confusion.

"Harry," Bruce said, "you know who I am."

Harry's eyes narrowed.

Bruce said, "I am your brother."

Harry rocked backward. He released his grip and Rob slumped forward, wheezing and clutching his neck.

Bruce said, "Come on, Rob. Thisaway." Rob crawled across the floor on his hands and knees to his father's side. Bruce did not embrace his son but pointed with his own chin down the hall behind him and clicked his tongue like he was directing an animal. "To bed now."

Rob obeyed.

As soon as Bruce's body was situated between his son's and his brother's—the immediate threat defused—he was flooded with so much relief he nearly collapsed.

Bruce could tell from the sounds behind him that Rob had not returned to his own bedroom but had gone instead to Bruce and Janet's.

Harry was trembling. "I get turned around sometimes. Especially at night. Certain things spark a response. I swear I woke to him rifling through my bag, just there. That doesn't matter. And, but, so, I got used to sleeping light back in service and never got over that. When I woke just now and saw someone scrambling through my things, in the dark and a place I didn't immediately know ... Things in my head weren't right. I wasn't here; he wasn't who he is; I wasn't who I am."

Bruce didn't know what to say to clear the air of this darkness.

He knew his brother had been through a lot. He'd heard of shell shock. And Rob, the cocky little sneak, probably was going through Harry's things, trying to recover some of the cash he had foolishly forfeited earlier in the evening. And yet. There was no returning from the threat posed to Rob's life, no escaping the shock of it, and no instant solution to the violence it had ignited in Bruce. A strange thought reached Bruce: if Harry had killed Rob—regardless of whether the inciting incident was based on a lie or a truth—Bruce would have killed Harry. Without a single consideration to the contrary. Bruce was certain he was capable of this, physically and otherwise.

But everything was calm and settled now, so why was he thinking about anybody killing anybody?

Harry rubbed his fingers over his face, looking mortified and aggrieved. He said, "I'll be going, then. Can't be staying after this.

What would Janet say?" Harry didn't look like he actually expected a response to this, and Bruce was grateful.

Allowing his brother to leave felt like its own form of cruelty. But Harry had risen and was readying his things to go. Bruce thought of things he could say, but none of them made it out.

Bruce watched out the window as his brother limped through snow to his car. Then Harry was gone.

In the bedroom Janet was sitting upright with her arms wrapped around Rob, who looked large next to her, especially considering how small he had looked under Harry's grip minutes earlier. It struck Bruce that in the living room Rob had undoubtedly been a child, but now, safe in his mother's arms, he could easily be mistaken for a man.

Janet said, "Is he gone?"

Bruce nodded.

"Thank God," Janet gasped. "What on earth?"

"It's since the war," Bruce said wearily. "He gets turned around sometimes."

"Well." Janet smoothed the blanket. "You did the right thing, telling him to leave."

Bruce didn't respond.

Janet said, "Attacking Rob? Nearly suffocating him, out of nowhere? Rob said he was just on his way to the kitchen?" She posed this as enough of a question that Bruce thought she might believe it warranted confirming.

Bruce found he could not meet his son's eyes as Rob piped up to insist, "It's true."

Bruce said, "I'm gonna go put the couch back together."

He did so, then sat in the living room by himself for some time.

He was not eager to return to the company of his wife and son for some reason, even though they were probably asleep and—thank God, thank God!—they were definitely alive. Of course it was right that Harry should leave. And about Rob. Bruce was somber and tormented as he grappled with uncertainty about his son's character. He had the strange notion that on the day Rob was born, holding Rob for the first time, Bruce knew both infinitely more and infinitely less about his son than he did now.

Bruce finally managed to get himself feeling a little better and then eventually to sleep, with the decision that he'd call Harry tomorrow to make sure Harry had gotten home all right and to make sure he knew he'd be welcome another time. It was just sort of too bad how this had gone, but Bruce wasn't mad. He'd say all of those things to Harry, tomorrow.

But Harry didn't pick up the phone when Bruce called the next day.

Bruce finally reached him a few days after that. He found that he wasn't quite able to say the things he'd hoped to but was relieved to confirm that his brother was home safely and they were still on speaking terms.

A few months later, Harry died in a car crash. No other vehicles were involved.

Janet said, "Poor man should've gotten the help he needed."

Corinne, who had not been told the full story because she was too young, said, "He left our house before we even did presents."

Rob said, "I was just going to the kitchen for something to eat."

Bruce said nothing.

All of this buckled painfully through Bruce. He couldn't seem to stick to any one way of feeling about the loss of his brother and their final moments together. Sometimes guilt sawed at Bruce, as he was sure he was responsible for Harry's death, thinking if he'd shown more compassion or called more times, said all the things he'd wanted to or some different things, or insisted Harry stay at his home regardless of how Janet and Rob felt about it, then Harry would still be alive. Sometimes Bruce felt angry at Harry for coming to stay at his home in the first place, knowing he was prone to these moments of confusion. Sometimes he felt angry about the war. Sometimes he thought car accidents were simply accidents.

More ongoing trouble was that Bruce was not able to look at his son's lying eyes ever since that night.

Time passed; Rob grew into a man; he left home; he made decisions, made money, and so forth. Once Rob left home it was impossible for Bruce to know the extent of his son's lies, but there were enough that were plainly obvious that Bruce lost track and lost the ability to hope for truth from his son. From time to time Janet brought up Rob's lies, though she harbored a rosier outlook than Bruce. Determined to maintain her opinion that they had raised their children well enough to be above such things, she was willing

to write off every lie Rob told as either a mistake or a miscommu-
nication or a harmless exaggeration, as she herself was prone to do.

It was hard for Bruce to hear other men talk about their adult
sons as though they were good friends.

The boundless love Bruce had for his son, of course, did not
change; the love was factual and resolved. But love was not the
only thing between men. There were other elements—approval,
trust, admiration—that floundered. For some time Bruce felt
powerless within his own heart to revisit or reclaim these things
where Rob was concerned. And in the presence of uncondi-
tional love, the absence of respect, for instance, was a staggering
conundrum.

But some sort of miracle happened a number of years later: at a
certain point, Bruce stopped caring about Rob's lying, including
the big one involving Harry. He couldn't pinpoint anything that
precipitated this shift; one day he simply realized he was so tired of
carrying the bad feeling toward Rob that he would carry it no longer. He thought, *The next time I see my son, I will believe him.* Somehow, suddenly, this faith required nothing of Bruce. He thought, *I
will feel joy to be together.*

But the next time Rob was home, when Bruce found that finally he was able to look clearly and squarely at his son's face, he
realized that Rob was not looking back at him. Bruce wondered,
Had the damage been done? Had Rob tried and failed to find his
father's eyes so many times these past few years that he had decided it was no longer worth trying?

The idea that Rob had given up trying to be properly seen and heard by his father was so painful that Bruce could hardly bear it. It was so painful that, once again, Bruce had to look away.

Janet had pointed out a number of times in relation to Bruce's mental decline that Bruce seemed not to recognize his son, peering at Rob like he was a complete stranger. Janet didn't seem to make much of this except to say that it was weird. "After all," she said, "you still seem to recognize everybody at church even if you can't come up with a name."

The thought of Janet and the smell of lemon Pledge is what brought Bruce back to the living room. The memories twisted and dissolved like a plume of smoke. Here was sunlight on the orange afghan spread over his thighs. The weight and the grip of his glasses over his nose.

Bruce looked down at the journal in his lap and read: *Janet, a gift from God.* He gazed at her, on the couch. He had no clue what she had done to inspire such high praise. Nevertheless, there she was, her little face pinched in concentration over her *People* magazine: his gift from God.

Bruce looked back down to examine the words again. It was his handwriting, and in fact he was still gripping the pen, so these words—foreign as they looked now—must have been generated by him, just moments earlier. But did he even believe in God if he could free himself of the notion that he ought to? Bruce's eyes drifted sleepily over the words as they skated around his brain.

His chin bobbled with fresh fatigue. Words, words, what a

nuisance. Even when accurate, words tumbled so far from any real truth that they might as well all be discarded as lies.

His eyelids drooped as he tried to focus, and the words swirled over the page:

Janet, a gift from God.
Janet, drifts through a fog.
Janet, a fig for a dog.

Bruce was so close to sleep now that none of these made any more or any less sense than any other.

Then, sleep flung its full heft upon him and he surrendered and was lost in the ocean of his life—swimming, struggling, wistful, wishing, grateful, tired, floating, fighting, cowering, drowning, wondering, wandering, worrying, doubting, grieving, grudging, thinking, praying, trapped, freed, forgiving, forgiven, searching, flowing, loving, loving; oh, how he loved. Was it okay not to be saying it, if he'd been doing it? Oh, how he'd tried, and oh, how he'd loved.

DECEMBER 1995

PART 2

EVEN AFTER OLIVIA BEGAN TO SLEEP LONGER STRETCHES, Corinne's body was still acclimated to hourly wake-ups, so she often found herself awake in the night while the baby slept. When this was the case and she had no other need to attend to except the settling of her own self, there were moments when the language of her unconscious asserted itself onto waking thought.

One snowy night Corinne dreamed, or imagined, that there was peace between herself and every person she had ever and would ever encounter, including the ones that had forgotten her and the ones that recalled every punishing detail. Then not only did she imagine this but she felt it too, and in this instant she realized that never before in her waking life had she even understood the meaning of this word, *peace*; entire oceans existed between her and it.

DECEMBER 1995

PART 3

AFTER MANY HOURS OF YAHTZEE, EUCHRE, BUSCH LIGHTS, TV, snacks, sweets, naps, gossip, and family photos, Janet served the Christmas Eve meal. They were six plus the baby, since Rob's twins were with their mother and he was accompanied instead by his girlfriend, Kai. Paul had observed the dynamic between Janet and Kai with amusement over the course of the day—Janet seemed desperate to ingratiate herself with Kai, following her around like a lapdog to offer up raw vegetables and over-the-top compliments.

After the meal, Janet and Corinne started working on mulled wine in the kitchen, and everyone else moved to the living room.

Paul paced and swayed with Olivia as she slept in his arms. They had reached an understanding in recent weeks: she would tolerate being held by him as long as he was standing and moving in the exact manner that she specified. Corinne was allowed to sit down while holding Olivia; this presented no issue. If Paul so much as thought about relaxing, Olivia went ballistic. Nowadays, instead of "She hates me" when Corinne passed Olivia his way, Paul said, "On your feet, soldier!"

Rob sat in the corner of the sectional with his feet propped up. Kai was sprawled elegantly across his lap, like a sleepy greyhound.

Bruce cleaned his glasses on the hem of his sweater, got his coat from the closet, and said to the room, "I'm going to go wish the Murphys a merry Christmas."

Rob said, "Who?"

"New neighbors."

"You're walking? It's freezing out. Twenty-some the last I checked and it wasn't dark yet. Dad, you haven't even got your hat."

"I've got this hood."

"They're not far, are they?"

"Nope." Bruce grunted up some phlegm, and out he went.

Rob said "Okey dokey" to the closed door and drank some beer.

When Paul passed the large front window on his next lap around the room with Olivia, he gazed out front. Bruce was already out of sight. Snow was swirling from side to side. He had a moment of concern for Bruce, who had not seemed like himself today, but then thought Bruce was probably just creating an excuse to escape Janet's domain for a while.

Rob turned on the TV and flipped absently through channels for a while, then handed the remote control to Kai. He got up, went to the woodstove, peered in. He retrieved a log from the stack against the wall, picked up kindling from the box nearby, balled up some sheets of newspaper, lit a few matches, and blew into the stove until the tinder caught.

Paul watched this process in a daze as he walked and patted Olivia's back, dipped, hummed, squatted, swayed.

Rob returned to the sectional, and Kai returned to his lap.

Paul could hear Janet and Corinne talking in the kitchen about a second cousin who'd had an eleven-pound baby. He walked and walked, enjoying Olivia's weight in his arms, her feather-soft hair against his neck, her open mouth, her breath that somehow smelled like both vinegar and sugar.

Janet entered the living room and wiped her hands on her apron. "Taking dessert orders," she said. "German chocolate cake or vegan apple crisp. Or both. And vanilla ice cream or whipped cream. And coffee?" She looked around the room. "Bruce on the toilet?"

Rob yawned. "He's not back yet? It's been a while now. He went to go wish the new neighbors a merry Christmas."

Janet's chin lowered ominously. "The new neighbors?"

"I thought it was unlike Dad, too," Rob said. "Making a visit unannounced like that. And it's so dang cold. But he said. The Murphys or something?"

Paul could sense from Janet's reaction that this was not a small matter. He wondered what Janet's issue was with these Murphys.

Janet stared out the front window, at the snow. "You let him go out in this? How long ago?"

Rob directed a defensive look at Paul to point out that he, too, had okayed the walk.

Paul said, "Maybe half an hour?"

"The hell!" A jagged artery bulged at Janet's temple.

Corinne appeared from around the corner.

Janet said, "These guys let your father go out wandering in this weather!" She flung her hand in the direction of the front lawn.

"What makes you think he's wandering around?" Rob said.

"The new neighbors probably just invited him to stay for a beer. Dad's a big boy, he'll be fine."

"There are no new neighbors," Janet barked. She untied her apron behind her, then pulled it off with a whipping sound.

Rob said, "Then who—"

Corinne said, "What is going on?"

Janet exploded: "Your father's losing it! His memory. His mind. He acts like it's his hearing. We were going to tell you all sooner, but things just kept getting in the way. He's losing it! Cuckoo! And now he's wandering around out there in this—this—this—what is it, *zero* degrees out there? Oh my God. For crying out loud!"

The next few moments occurred in thunderclaps. Panic whizzed through the room. Confusion and despair and accusations were leveled but abandoned in deference to logistics and the emergency at hand.

Decisions were made: Corinne would stay at the house with Olivia since it was far too cold for the baby to be out. She would dial the neighbors whose numbers Janet had. If none of them had seen Bruce and if no one from the family had returned within half an hour to inform her that Bruce had been found, she was to call the cops. The rest of them would divide and conquer in the meantime. Rob and Janet would head out in their vehicles to canvass the neighborhood as quickly as possible, knocking on doors. Paul and Kai would go in separate directions but on foot, in case his tracks were not yet fully blown over or he'd strayed from the road. Once Bruce was found, someone would round up everyone still out looking.

After dressing for the frigid weather, Paul and Kai walked down the driveway together. It was very windy and no tracks were visible. Paul would go left; Kai, right.

Before parting ways Kai said, "I thought it was obvious the man was struggling cognitively. Didn't you?"

Cold air licked Paul's cheeks and echoed powerfully in his ears. He couldn't respond right away because emotion had gathered like glue in his throat. He made an O of his mouth to release some sculpted clouds.

Kai added, "You've known Bruce a lot longer than me. What do you think?"

Paul was thinking how self-centered and obtuse he must be not to have noticed, about this man he loved, what was immediately obvious to Kai. Accompanying this thought was the comforting revelation that he loved Bruce. Not just as an extension of his love for Corinne but as love that stood fully on its own two feet. Paul thought of his own father and wondered about the basis and sturdiness of that love. Then he thought of Bruce again.

He said, "I couldn't say."

Paul walked along the road. A frozen layer of thick slush crunched beneath his feet. He gazed at homes that were filled with light and some that were dark and shuttered. Rob was moving quickly ahead of him, zipping in and out of driveways, and once he was out of sight Paul gauged his progress from the tracks left by Rob's SUV.

Up and down the blocks Paul trudged.

Eventually it had been half an hour, then more. He had not seen or heard rescue vehicles but was far enough from their home by now that he thought they could have come and gone without his notice.

Then, it had been an hour. Paul's mind felt cramped.

He thought of Corinne and Olivia and wondered how things were going for them back at the house. Despite the superficial monotony of their lives, things were changing so quickly. Every day, different things became easier or harder. Difficult things early on were Olivia's refusal to settle for Paul, her gas, poor sleep for all of them. Now, difficult things were the rashes on her chin and bottom. Someday, Paul knew, all of these difficulties would be distant memories and the new and permanent difficult thing would be Olivia outgrowing her need for him.

Paul could not rid himself entirely of his trivial daily concerns or his unflagging pessimism, which for his entire life had shoehorned its way into every happiness. Yet lately his darkness had lost his teeth, since some weeks ago he had found that he was able to make his wife laugh again. His jokes had either gotten better or Corinne was actually listening. Either way, they had found each other in the fog. Or perhaps it was not that they had gotten lost in it, or even moved a single inch away from each other, but the fog had merely lifted, and there they still were.

At a few minutes past the hour mark, Paul turned to head back, thinking that by now authorities would have surely been alerted and his ongoing efforts here were of no use.

Shortly after he'd turned around, headlights appeared, approached, and Rob lowered the window of his SUV to wave Paul in.

Paul shivered violently as he settled onto the passenger seat. The heat in the car felt like liquid gold poured onto his numb face.

Rob said, "I found him on the ground a few blocks away, halfway up some stranger's lawn. Sorry it took a while for me to get to you—I had to deal with the paramedics, then round up Mom and Kai."

"Is he okay?"

"He was totally out of it when I found him. Maybe some frost-bite. Maybe a stroke. We don't know anything, really. He's on his way to the hospital, or there by now."

Paul breathed warm air into his gloved hands.

Rob sniffed like he might be crying.

"Hey, I'm sorry," Paul said, and he stared straight ahead.

"Dads, man."

Back at the house, Kai was taking a hot shower and Corinne had just gotten off the phone with her mother. Janet had called from the hospital to report that Bruce was stable but they needed to run many tests and would be there for the night, maybe longer. They thought he'd had a stroke and did not know what this would look like in terms of his memory and cognition on the other side.

Corinne said, "They're in room 376 at the hospital if we need to reach them. She'll keep us posted. She said we should rest up and wait to visit till the morning. She said we could come anytime tomorrow, just to call first."

Rob shed his layers, poured himself a whiskey, and sat on the couch.

Olivia was awake and fussing. Paul took her from Corinne and began to sway.

Corinne sank into the La-Z-Boy and stared out the window. She said, "I thought it was just part of getting old. Stumbling over a name, staring off."

Olivia was active now, so Paul dipped lower, faster.

Corinne's voice sharpened. "I am so pissed at Mom. I tried to be nice on the phone. Now's not the time to pile on. But God!" She let out a puff of air.

Paul said, "For not telling you sooner?"

"She stole all of his final lucid months. Hoarded all of them for

herself. Actively throwing us off the scent with the hearing business." She reached down to pull the lever on the La-Z-Boy to elevate the footrest and lurched backward. "Most of the time I think
she's annoying but harmless. Then this."

Rob was bent over his whiskey and swirling it slowly.

Paul didn't know what to say. He thought about piping up to
agree that, yes, sometimes the people you love are terrible or distant or cruel or otherwise harmful in ways that cannot be understood or explained away. He didn't say this though, because it was
no consolation whatsoever; it offered nothing but a depressing
fact.

Rob said, "I'm just surprised it wasn't obvious to you, even
with the efforts to hide it. You being here in town and all."

Corinne scowled at her brother. "I suppose it wouldn't have
gone unnoticed all this time if you were here to see it."

"Mom says she barely sees you even though you're only ten
minutes away."

"You are more than welcome to move back home anytime,
whenever you want, to lend a hand with Mom and Dad. Since
you're obviously the best one for the task."

When Rob didn't argue, Corinne continued, "I'm dead serious. Come back home, why don't you? What's keeping you there?
Name one thing. One person. Other than Kai."

"Wow." Rob looked at his sister darkly. "Screw you."

"You went there first, implying I'm a bad daughter."

"Did not."

"You didn't come right out and say it but you're skirting close.
You know, you're good at that. Skirting around things. You're a
hard one to pin right down, Robbie. Always have been. Hard to get
a straight answer from you."

"You know what?" Rob took a breath through his nose and spoke evenly. "Kai has really helped me see things clearly. She's opened my eyes, to me, about myself."

"Don't make me beg for this insight."

"I can already tell from your tone that you're going to say something insulting."

"I've got the openest mind."

"Kai is the first person I've ever met who sees me for the good person that I am. Beneath the bullshit. She sees my good heart. The rest of you don't see that. You only see what's on the surface."

Paul stole a glance at Corinne, who blinked slowly, dumbly. She said, "So the bullshit doesn't matter then? Only the intangibles underneath? How wonderful that you found someone who shares such a generous and enlightened perspective about your essence."

"I knew it was only a matter of time till you shat all over my love."

"Your love?"

"Kai and her spiritual gifts."

"I'm not shitting on Kai," Corinne said. "I actually really like her. I think she's great for you."

Rob poured the rest of his whiskey into his mouth and grimaced through the swallow.

Kai entered the room wearing silk pajamas. She was squeezing water from her long hair into a towel. No one spoke. She said, "Anybody need anything?" and took a seat when nobody did. She broke an uncomfortable silence to say to Rob, "Your dad brought up his brother, Harry, earlier today. Is he still living? I didn't remember ever hearing about him."

Corinne said, "Rob hasn't told you about Uncle Harry? Big surprise."

"Why would you say it like that?" Rob snapped at his sister, then turned to Kai. "Uncle Harry died in a car wreck. And before that, he almost killed me. I was fifteen years old. He jumped me and was this close to strangling me." He jabbed his thumbs into his throat.

"No need to be so dramatic," Corinne said.

"You weren't even there," Rob said.

"But I've heard the story." Corinne explained to Kai: "Harry served in the war. Came home with PTSD. He spent Christmas here one year and got confused in the night when he woke to Rob going through his bags, trying to swipe some cash or something. He died not long after that, and it seemed like it might not have been an accident."

Rob's jaw fell open. "I was just going to the kitchen for something to eat!"

Corinne arched her brows.

"Who told you I was lying?" Rob demanded.

"I can't remember if it was Mom or Dad who told me the story. I'm sure I heard it from both of them at some point. And I actually can't remember what they said about you lying anyway. They might not have even mentioned that; I might have just assumed, after hearing the other facts. And considering your track record."

Paul had heard the Uncle Harry story some time ago from Corinne and tried now to recall who had determined that Rob was lying, but he couldn't remember if Rob's lie was even included in the version of the story that Corinne had told or if he had simply drawn the conclusion himself.

"I still have nightmares about the experience," Rob said. "The threat to my life. I can't believe you're making this about some hypothetical lie I supposedly told versus Harry practically murdering me. He was so close. I would have been a goner. You'd be the sister of a murder victim. You'd probably love that, wouldn't you?"

Corinne said, "I'm just saying that Uncle Harry probably wouldn't have attacked you if you hadn't been going through his things. And if it hadn't happened at all, maybe he would have stayed for the holiday and everything would have turned out different."

Rob stared at her. "I cannot believe you're defaulting to the idea that I lied and that you even think that's an important part of this story. For God's sake! Does no one care about my life?"

Kai said, "I'm sorry I brought—"

Corinne did not seem to register Kai's presence in the room. She said to Rob, "What do you mean no one cares about your life? What—who—are you even talking about?"

Paul noticed that Rob's face was now puffy and red, like Janet's got sometimes. Rob said, "Did you know that Dad wouldn't look at me that night when I tried to talk to him? The most terrifying experience of my life, and Dad wouldn't even look at my face? Like he would have just let something—anything—happen, because he didn't know who to believe and was too busy deliberating to see the threat before him? Do you know what that does to a kid, to know their father doesn't believe them, might not even defend them, in a moment like that?" Rob took a gasping inhale, then burst forth with more emotion: "Everybody thinks Dad is such a saint because he never loses his temper or breathes a word of criticism, or okay, so Dad probably never tells lies either—because he never says anything at all. That doesn't mean he wasn't capable of hurting me. Changing me. Just because he didn't accuse me outright of lying doesn't mean I didn't feel accused. Just because he never outright blamed me for Harry's death doesn't mean I didn't feel blamed. Does that make sense to you now?"

Corinne blinked, then asked in a measured tone, "But, Rob, were you lying?"

Rob's eyes popped wide in indignation at this continued line of questioning.

Even Paul, who had never once sided with Rob over his wife in an argument, thought maybe Corinne should lay off.

Rob said, "What difference does that make? I was a child, my life was threatened, and I swore to my father I was telling the truth!"

"But were you?"

"What?"

"Telling the truth?"

Rob exploded, "What difference does it make?"

"The whole difference!" Corinne roared back. "If he was right about you lying, then where do you get off being upset about the accusation?"

Olivia woke to the sound of her mother's angry voice and started to howl. Paul was relieved for the distraction. He had never witnessed things go this far between the siblings and didn't know what came next.

Rob slammed his whiskey glass onto the table. "I'll tell you one thing," he said. "I will never in my life look away from my boys. Let me be the idiot! I will never torture them with silence."

Corinne scoffed. "The idea of Dad torturing anyone, ever, with *silence* of all things—"

"I'd rather someone tell me something, anything, or punish me in any kind of way, than just stop looking at me," Rob said. "Maybe you and I are different that way, though. Maybe you prefer someone just look away any time there's any sort of issue. Actually, I guess it all makes sense." Rob's tone was snotty, obnoxious.

"What's that supposed to mean?" Corinne said.

Rob tipped his head vaguely in Paul's direction. The implication was not immediately clear to Paul, but Corinne responded with fury. "You're going to insult my husband and my marriage now? That's rich. Just because Paul doesn't talk to *you* doesn't mean he doesn't talk to me."

Paul could not believe he had been roped into this fight. He knew Rob was just going for cheap shots, that regardless of how rosy things were with Kai, Rob would probably give anything to still be married to Liz—and Corinne's happiness made him so jealous he could not help himself. Still, Paul could not let this slide. Could he? No, he thought, he'd better not; staying quiet now would merely prove Rob's point.

Paul spoke firmly but quietly enough that it would not disturb Olivia: "Hey, Rob, fuck you."

Rob cupped his hand around his ear. "What?"

Paul thought for a second that his brother-in-law might be trying to goad him into a physical altercation but then realized from Rob's expression that Rob actually had not heard what he'd said and was asking Paul, in earnest, to repeat himself.

Paul walked a little closer. He leaned toward Rob and whispered, over Olivia's head: "I said, fuck you."

Rob said, "Oh." He looked genuinely hurt. Definitely not like he wanted to fight.

Nearby, Corinne started to crack up. She had picked up a notebook in the magazine rack next to the La-Z-Boy where she sat and was laughing at whatever she had discovered inside. She pointed and read out loud, "'Janet, a gift from God.' In Dad's writing."

"Oh, hell," Rob said. "He really has lost it."

Corinne was crying and laughing, and Rob brought her a Kleenex.

He offered one to Paul too, and when Paul declined, Rob grabbed his shoulder and said, "We good?"

Paul was so weary he found himself unable to access anger or even his normal baseline irritation with Rob. "Sure," he said.

Looking at the presents beneath Bruce and Janet's mangy artificial tree, Paul wondered if Corinne was planning on doing some sort of Santa routine with Olivia in future years, once she was old enough to enjoy that sort of thing. They hadn't discussed this yet. He knew that Corinne had believed in Santa for a good many Christmases and was crushed to intercept Bruce with the presents in the middle of the night one year.

Paul had never believed, despite his mother's best efforts, and his father seemed to consider Paul's lack of faith a point of pride.

Olivia squirmed in Paul's arms and turned away from his chest in order to locate her mother in the room. Once she had confirmed Corinne's proximity, she was satisfied to settle back into Paul. Her limbs became weighty, and Paul, too, was so tired he felt like he could collapse with each step, yet he kept walking even as his muscles ached with fatigue and his thoughts failed to reach meaningful destinations.

He looked at Corinne. "Sorry," he said. "Did you say something?"

"I said we need to call your mother."

Ellen was surprised to hear from Paul at eight thirty on Christmas Eve, since they had already spoken earlier in the day.

She listened as Paul told her about Bruce being lost and found and out of it and hospitalized, and, as it turned out, deteriorating mentally for quite some time. "So Corinne is nervous about leaving town with her dad in the hospital," Paul explained.

"Of course." Ellen braced herself.

"She wondered if you would want to drive up and be here for Christmas Day instead, so she could stay close to Bruce in case anything happens and so we could visit him sometime tomorrow." Paul waited a beat, then added, "If you're open to coming here, maybe you'd even want to make the drive tonight, so we'd have the full day together tomorrow. We'd make the bed up, have everything ready for you tonight. Try and have a nice Christmas here. I know it's not what you were hoping for."

Ellen opened her refrigerator to stare at the neat stack of Tupperwares that held all of the food for tomorrow. Everything was labeled—not just with what it contained but with how long and at what temperature it needed to go in.

She said, "You know what I'll do, I'll pack everything into a cooler so we can all still enjoy it tomorrow. But then there is still the issue of your father. We were all going to be . . . so that . . . for your sake . . ."

"You wanted Dad to be at Christmas for *my* sake?"

"I just pictured this year being like your Christmases growing up. Perfect, like that. For Olivia's first."

"You think our Christmases were perfect? Dad was always in a terrible mood. Brooding about. Criticizing your every move. And you were always trying and failing to cheer him up, thinking if you got the meal just right he'd be happy, and all your efforts just made things worse." Paul paused. "Just like every other day of the year."

Ellen blinked in pain and disbelief. "That's not true, Paul. You're so wrong. We were all enjoying ourselves! We were all happy."

"No, *you* were happy. Somehow."

"What were you?"

"I guess I was watching."

One sob whirled its way up and down Ellen's spine but it made no sound.

Paul said, "I was prepared to tolerate Dad's presence tomorrow for your sake. But how could you possibly want that? Maybe you're over it. Him leaving. Or maybe you're still hoping. Mom, are you still hoping?"

"To get back together?"

"Yes."

Ellen thought. What did it matter, what she wanted? When had it ever mattered, even to her?

Paul spoke again before she could. He said bluntly, "I think Dad is dating again. Or has. Or is trying. I don't know who or how many. He'll claim that it was never about another woman, but I think that's just because he knows you're less likely to start dating if you think he's not. I think it was always about other women for him. Options. Attempts. Younger, probably? Conquests. I'm not trying to be mean. I'm trying to make you see how he actually is. I think he says 'drifted apart' because that keeps 'drifting back' on the table. Mom, I think what he's doing to you is unbelievably cruel."

Ellen was too stunned to speak.

Paul said again, "I'm not trying to be mean. I don't know any of this for a fact, because he won't talk to me. Whatever the case, I'll be happier not seeing him tomorrow, and I think you will be, too. All along I've been sort of hoping there would be a change of plans anyway; like at some point you'd say it was Gary going to be there tomorrow. Someone else, anyone, instead of Dad."

Ellen felt her chin snap back reflexively. "How do you know Gary?"

"He's the one that made Olivia the abacus, isn't he?"

Ellen thought back. She had delivered the wrapped gift back when Olivia was born but had intentionally not specified whether it was a man or woman who had made the gift. She didn't know if Paul harbored hopes of her reconciling with Michael and didn't want to assume Paul would view a new relationship favorably. She had thought she definitely would not want to be dating before Michael was.

Paul said, "It was such an incredible gift, I assumed it had to be from someone who was trying to impress you."

"How did you know his name?"

"The card inside."

Ellen realized she had delivered the gift but not been there when they opened it. "We could hardly believe it was from someone we didn't even know."

Ellen said, "What did it say?"

"The card? The normal stuff. Congratulations. How he can't wait to meet her."

Ellen felt a sad crashing recognition.

Paul continued, "I have no idea what your relationship is. And I assume he has his plans for tomorrow. But if he wants to come to ours for Christmas or any other time, I'd be happy to meet him. And I know you don't mind being on the road in the dark and with snow, but some company might be nice for the drive."

Ellen tried to make sense and make room for this revelation: Paul's feelings, her feelings. Was nothing sacred, nothing solid? How could it be that one vision, a hope, could dissolve so unceremoniously? How dare a new hope rise so swiftly and so dangerously to her surface to replace it? How dare life surprise her yet again?

She said, "Last we talked, Gary wasn't going to see his daughter till the twenty-sixth and he was dreading his plans on Christmas Day. But, honey, it's so weird. I'm sure he won't come. He probably won't even pick up the phone. Or if he does, he might hang up when he knows it's me. It's a long story."

"Do what you want about Gary," Paul said. "But let me be the one to call Dad. I'll explain about Bruce and tell him the plan's changed and tomorrow at your house is off. You just get yourself here safely. You've got our house key. We'll have the guest room made up, like always."

After hanging up, Ellen looked at the ceramic Nativity set that she always put out as a centerpiece on the kitchen table. Paul had dropped the baby Jesus one year, and the head had had to be re-glued many times since. She picked up Jesus and examined him closely. After all the repairs, his neck had become very elongated and he resembled E.T. She turned him around in the light and said out loud, "You poor thing, you've really been through the wringer. Maybe it's time we put you out of your misery."

Paul dialed his father's number right away. He felt prepared for whatever sort of reaction his father would have to the change of plans, whether it was self-pity or anger or a creative alternative option that still had him joining the group, which Paul was prepared to rebuff.

So when a woman picked up the phone at his father's house, Paul almost laughed; this he had not prepared for.

She didn't offer a name, just a "Hello?"

Paul said, "Is Michael there? My dad. This is his son."

"Sure, honey," she said. "He's just in the other room."

Paul thought she sounded possibly drunk, possibly from the South, and possibly surprised to learn that Michael had a son.

He heard the receiver plunk onto a hard surface, some shuffling about, then his father's voice.

"Paul," Michael said.

"Hi, Dad."

His father's breath crackled into the receiver. "Listen," Michael said, and Paul could tell from the whispered tone and boosted volume that his father had now cupped his free palm around the mouthpiece so that Paul could hear him better and his houseguest could not hear at all.

"I'm listening," Paul said.

"With her," Michael whispered, "it's not serious. Ahem. I'm hoping tomorrow's still on. Right? This was just, she's nothing. I was feeling sorry for myself, alone on Christmas Eve."

"Tomorrow is off," Paul said curtly. "Nothing to do with you. Bruce had a medical emergency and Mom's driving up to be here."

"Oh," Michael said flatly. "Okay. But just so we're clear, like I said, the gal who answered—"

Paul interrupted, "I don't care." He was quiet for a bit, then said, "Actually, I do."

Hours earlier Bruce had left the house with the idle notion that a short walk in the snow would clear his head. He was uncomfortably full of food and overwhelmed by a day of festivities. He told the people in the living room, which included his son, Rob, and some woman with a newfangled name Bruce couldn't remember, that he would be back soon. They did not press him for details, so he thought he must have managed to say something normal. All day, Janet had been whispering at Bruce to *just act normal!* She had always fancied herself an authority on this matter, and he had little choice but to trust her, especially nowadays when so often he did not feel like himself.

Bruce hadn't intended to go far at all. But once he was outside in the dark, away from Janet and gripped instead by a rather shocking cold, his mind broke apart into pieces. All the facts changed.

The new facts were these: Harry needed help, and Bruce had to get to the nearest house as fast as he could to find it.

Bruce traipsed through snow, heaving for breath, his whole body prickling with cold. *Must hurry*, he thought. His joints felt like all bone on bone, nothing soft. Cold mucus clumped at his nostrils.

Soon enough he saw golden lights on a porch and was reassured—it was a small, kindly-looking brick house. He didn't recognize it but was sure he must know its occupants, since they were neighbors. His mind was zooming through different timelines. *Faster now!* he urged his aching legs. *Find someone, anyone, who can help Harry.* He trudged doggedly ahead.

But despite his intentions and determination, Bruce's mind kept jerking back to the grotesque sight of Harry's injured foot and his anguished face so that eventually Bruce could not separate his brother's pain from his own, and he stumbled.

He attempted to will himself up and forward, and when his body failed him and he found himself immobilized in the snow, he tried to call for help, but his voice went nowhere, devoured at once by the frigid air that met his lips.

Bruce's thoughts were sliding down like hot wax. Things had

gone so dark they were nearly going light. He listened for music but instead heard the voice of his son: "Oh my God! Dad! Hey, hey. Dad, look at me. Come on. Stay with me."

Although he could not look or see, Bruce was suddenly lucid, heart roaring with love, and he thought: *It doesn't matter what's between us, Robbie! There has not been a moment of your life when I wouldn't have died or killed to save you, Robbie! My child, how I love you!* Bruce knew that these words were artless and unoriginal but they were the sum, and this was the end. Or was it? Bruce wondered senselessly if, when it came to life, there were many endings but no actual ends—not even this one.

"Dad," Rob's voice came through again. "Oh, God. Stay with me. Are you still here?"

Bruce wasn't sure. So he kept listening to find out.

Gary had kept himself busy throughout the day with baking, decorating the tree, and wrapping gifts for his daughter and her girlfriend. Now that everything was ready for their arrival the day after tomorrow, he was worn out and starting to mentally prepare himself for the big meal at his cousin Susan's house tomorrow.

All things considered, things were going okay for Gary. He'd not returned to the divorce support group since October but had replaced it with weekly AA meetings. The day after Halloween, he'd given the bottle of port wine to his friend Lewis, who was celebrating a fortieth wedding anniversary.

He had not heard from Ellen since Halloween, and as the days passed, he thought it increasingly likely that Michael had weaseled his way back into her good graces. This hurt Gary to think about, so he tried not to think about it.

Gary sat down on the La-Z-Boy and had just turned on the television, when the phone rang. His back was sore and he almost decided not to get up to answer. He'd already spoken with all the family members he'd expect to hear from on Christmas Eve and thought the call must either be a misdial or a Pilar. He roused himself, though, and was surprised to find Ellen at the other end. She said, "I didn't know if I'd find you."

"Ho, ho, ho," he said.

"Do you have time to talk?"

"Let me get the cordless."

Gary retrieved his cordless phone and settled himself back down on the La-Z-Boy. He propped his feet up.

Ellen told him first about the situation with Bruce. Then she told him about her conversation with Paul and the revelation that Paul not only did not want to spend Christmas with his father but mentioned him—Gary—specifically and his hopes that perhaps his mother was dating. Ellen said, "I had things all turned around. What I wanted."

"How do you mean?"

"I think I only ever wanted what I thought my child wanted, and it turns out I didn't even get that right." She sighed. "I'm sure you have your plans. But last we talked, you were dreading the wingding at Susan's. I'm fixing to head to Paul and Corinne's place here in a few minutes, for the night and so that we have all day together tomorrow. I could come back whenever you wanted, depending when your daughter and her girlfriend get in. Now I know you and I haven't seen each other in months. This is so silly. I shouldn't even ask. Just, talking to Paul got me thinking. Oh my word, Gary. What a mess I've made. The support group thing threw me for a loop. I'm sorry."

"I'm sorry, too."

"What for?"

"Being such a stubborn son of a bitch that I didn't call you. I wanted to."

"I'm the one who left in a huff. I'm the one who made the mess."

"Water under the bridge," Gary said. If there was anything he'd learned from his divorce—and there was a lot, actually—it was that an eye was never for an eye, injuries were never equal, and comparing damage was useless.

"Well," Ellen said, "it seems like in the end, with Michael, it was that I wasn't sexy enough anymore. Or maybe I never was. I guess that was it?"

She paused, and for a moment Gary felt too sad to speak.

Ellen said, "You don't have to say so."

"I think you're the sexiest lady in the world," Gary said. "And if you're sure you're up for the company, then I guess Susan will have to survive tomorrow without my wit and good cheer."

"All right! I'll drive!" Ellen shouted at him. "I just need a few minutes to get packed. Oh, you'll probably want to bring that foam thing you sleep with, for your back. I'm gonna get myself together here, then I'll come to you."

The flurries had ended and the night sky was bright and clear.

Ellen was a much more aggressive driver than Gary would have guessed.

She always liked talking about her family, but tonight she seemed on a special mission. She chattered the whole way, telling Gary more about Paul and Corinne and baby Olivia than he could have ever imagined to ask. She kept saying, "When we're with them, you'll see," and then continuing to tell him what he would see.

In room 376 of the hospital, Janet was standing at the window, peering out at the low, yellow moon. This wing of the building overlooked a bare, uninterrupted view of new snow over frozen cornfields that spanned the whole way to the horizon.

Behind her, Bruce was hooked up to so many machines she couldn't bear to look at him.

Oh, she knew she was in the deep shit now. She knew her children would save their righteous indignation for the morning, when they'd all gotten rest. But she knew it was coming, and she knew she deserved it. But it's not like they were so perfect—Rob with his lies and Corinne with her superiority—and Janet would make sure they knew it.

One of Bruce's machines chirped and Janet did not turn to see why. She figured if it was anything important, it would do more than chirp.

Bruce's vitals were stable, but no one knew what was going on in his head. They would run a bunch of tests in the morning. The doctor had prepared Janet for the likelihood that Bruce would waken to considerable cognitive damage.

Janet had asked, "Will he know who I am?"

The doctor said there were no guarantees.

Janet was struck by the notion that, actually, there could be worse outcomes.

A more sobering thought followed: if Bruce did not know that he was bound to her, if he woke with no idea how he had gotten here or who he was—if he woke not merely confused but blank, his mind as empty as the day he was born—well, what would he make of Janet then? Would he choose her again, as he had forty-five years ago, if he was looking at her anew and believed he had a say in the matter?

Looking out over the golden moonlight that sailed across the endless expanse of untouched snow before her, Janet felt a powerful longing. At first she thought it was for life as it was forty-five years ago. But then she realized that her yearning went even further back, all the way back. She longed to wake as Bruce might tomorrow morning, to a blank slate, to everything new and unknown. She longed to find herself in someone's loving arms as she realized for the first time, in wonderment, in every language: I am a life!

Unable to sleep, Rob decided to pay his father a visit at the hospital in the middle of the night despite his mother's request that the children wait until morning and call ahead.

Rob had gotten to thinking that Corinne was absolutely right and Janet could not be trusted with vital information. As he lay awake in bed, he had become increasingly paranoid that his mother had not been truthful about his father's condition. Rob believed it was a distinct possibility that things were far worse than Janet had led them to believe; for all he knew, this could be his father's last night, his final hours. Was this, then, the ending? Bruce, there; Rob, here?

Desperation thundering through him at the idea of this, Rob got up, dressed for the cold, gave Kai a kiss, and drove.

He arrived at the hospital around midnight, outside of normal visitation hours, but the woman working reception took pity and permitted him entry after Rob showed his ID, told her of his father getting lost in the dark earlier that evening, and pointed out that it was Christmas. She directed him toward the three hundred wing.

As Rob shuffled down the dark and empty hall, his mind was on life and death.

He felt abject despair and hope and also, somehow, everything in between. It was hard to have a father. It was hard to be a father. It was hard to lose a father, whenever and however that happened. He passed a room with a voice howling out of it. This was not his father's room, but he was almost there. Rob's heart felt so big and so broken. If it were possible to feel every human emotion in one moment, now was that moment. One part of him begged another part: *Don't think. Don't think. Don't think.*

Corinne was awake when Gary and Ellen arrived, even though it was nearly midnight. She was sitting on a rocker with Olivia, who, Corinne explained, was refusing to settle in the crib. Corinne was wearing an oversized Bengals T-shirt and she looked extremely tired. The overhead lights were off—the only lights in the room were colored bulbs on the tree, which stood at a slight angle. The living room was small and cozy, filled with mismatched furniture and framed family photos. It smelled of cinnamon.

Ellen said, "Corinne, this is Gary."

Corinne shoved hair back from her face and said, "The abacus is beautiful. I'm so happy to meet you, Gary. Merry Christmas. The guest room's all set. Oh, except for the duvet cover, that's still sitting in the dryer. I'm so tired I can't even think straight. If you hold her for a minute, Ellen, I'll get the duvet ready for you."

Ellen said, "Don't worry about that, Corinne. We've got it.

How about if I hold her for a few hours while you try to sleep? I'm all wound up from the drive anyway; it will take me forever to fall asleep."

Corinne said, "Are you sure? I was going to get Paul up for a shift soon."

Olivia had wakened and was craning her neck to see the new faces in the room.

"No, you kids get some sleep," Ellen insisted. "We've got the duvet and the baby covered. Go to sleep now. Bye-bye." She held out her hands for Olivia. "Night-night," she urged Corinne. "Go on."

Once Corinne was gone, Ellen faced Olivia toward Gary. "Isn't she the prettiest baby you've ever seen?"

Olivia's eyes fixed on Gary. He was mesmerized.

Olivia blinked and then she smiled with one side of her mouth and Gary said, "Hah!"

Ellen moved to pass Olivia to Gary. He extended his arms, wanting to hold her but feeling nervous. He didn't want her to cry. He said, "I don't remember how to do this."

"You're doing perfect," Ellen said.

Once Olivia was in his arms, Gary remembered everything.

When his own daughter was a baby, she had demanded constant movement from him. Endless hours he spent on his feet with her. Day and night, never sitting, never still. She would raise hell if he paused his movement for two seconds to stretch his sore back. Gary was into Creedence Clearwater Revival at the time and liked to listen to "Walk on the Water" while holding her. It was a good tempo for a stroll and had a guitar solo that he never got tired of. He remembered his wife saying, "I wish you wouldn't play that creepy song for her." Gary remembered saying if he was holding the baby, he was choosing the music, period. How silly, he thought

now, how stubborn, like there were no other songs in the world
that he could enjoy. He remembered tormenting his wife by turning the music even louder, provoking her into a fight about the volume and the lyrics and angels of death and subliminal messages
and Lord knows what all else. Obviously, he thought now, he had
just been acting out to get his wife's attention. It was so hard to get
your wife's attention when there was a baby around.

He took Olivia to the front window and faced her out.

The neighbors across the street had a magnificently garish
Christmas display: colored lights circling the evergreens, an in-
flatable life-sized Santa, six reindeer. The moon was nearly full and
butter-yellow and it hung over their house like a strung-up prop; it
fit right in like it was part of their display.

Olivia arched her back and cried out. Gary instinctively dipped
his knees and swayed deeper to soothe her; it worked.

He felt recklessly, immoderately happy.

Would this moment flow and pass and disappear for some
time—like the memory of holding his own daughter—or for the
rest of time, like so many others? It could break his heart, he knew,
if he let it.

Outside, everything was shining and nothing was moving.

Gary kept swaying and he said to Olivia, "Look."

He couldn't think of anything else to say.

ACKNOWLEDGMENTS

Huge and heartfelt thanks to Michelle Tessler, Jack Shoemaker, Jane Vandenburgh, Megan Fishmann, Dan Smetanka, Alyson Forbes, Yukiko Tominaga, Rachel Fershleiser, Nicole Caputo, Laura Berry, Wah-Ming Chang, Dan López, and as always to my family, most especially my boys, who guide me and ground me and fill my days with joy. Oh, how I love you, little ones.

© Rachel Herr

REBECCA KAUFFMAN received her MFA in creative writing from New York University. She is the author of *Another Place You've Never Been*, which was long-listed for the Center for Fiction First Novel Prize; *The Gunners*, which received the Premio Tribùk dei Librai; *The House on Fripp Island*; and, most recently, *Chorus*. Originally from rural northeastern Ohio, Kauffman now lives in Virginia. Find out more at rebeccakauffman.net.